Losing Grace

BETSY LOVE

Other Books by Betsy Love

Identity
Soulfire
The Penny Project

StarBride Chronicles-series:
The Captain and the Healer's Heart
Falling for a Fraud
Surrogate Hearts
The Gravity of a Kiss
Elspeth's StarBrides

The Miracle of Joie

Mystics Tale Series:
The Dragon Keeper

How to:
Plotting for Pantsers in Six Easy Steps

Dedication

To all the moms who wished
they could go back and fix their mistakes

Acknowledgements

First and foremost, to my sweet husband who is my greatest idea man. and all-time fan He helps me come up with what happens next. His favorite phrase is "What if?" Most of the time, he is spot on!

To my children who taught me that being their mother doesn't mean I have to be perfect at it, although there are times I wish I could go back and fix the mistakes I made in raiding them. In spite of my parenting, they turned into great human beings.

To Jen Peters who got the first look at my manuscript and gave me invaluable feedback. Becky Rohner and Courtney Holton for their impeccable editing skills.

Also, a huge shout out to my daughter, Joy, who patiently kept changing my book cover until it was just right.

To my ANWA sisters (and now brothers are included as well), who have encouraged me to write and publish.

Last, but certainly not the least, is Marsha Ward, whose vision for the ANWA writer's organization has given me support over the years. We love you so much, and pray for you always.

Losing
Grace

1

Friday, December 13, 2019

Janae wasn't the first parent to lose a child in death, and she wouldn't be the last. She'd been told to move past it, to carry on, to find joy again. For Janae, Liliana's drowning had sucked all the life from her. She didn't know how she was ever going to make it through the holidays.

The alarm on her phone went off. Time to face another day without her daughter, again. She hit dismiss and rolled onto her back.

"Wake up, sunshine, or you're going to be late!"

Janae turned toward the wall and pulled the pillow over her ears. "Five more minutes."

"You don't have the luxury of five more minutes." Someone who sounded like her mother tapped her on the foot. What was she doing here?

Janae rubbed her eyes, they should have been swollen and puffy from crying herself to sleep. Odd... she just felt tired, not exhausted, as usual. She propped herself on her elbow.

This woman standing at the end of her bed looked like a much younger version of her mom, no wrinkles, no gray hair. A bright smile covered her face. "You have to be to work in thirty minutes."

Janae curled her feet up next to her like she was playing a game of hot lava with the kids. "I don't have a job."

"Oh, but you do." She pulled a pair of black slacks out of a tiny closet near the foot of the bed and draped them on the end.

Where had the footboard gone, the decorative one with the maple finish? "Where am I, and who are you?" Had her husband drugged her and dragged her out of the house and put her in some sleazy motel? She knew her husband was angry with her when she'd turned him away last night, but he wouldn't resort to something this harsh, would he? He'd never done that before, so why start now?

She gazed at the kitchenette a few feet away. It held a single sink, a small fridge, hotplate, and toaster. Under the counter was a single drawer and cupboard.

Falling back onto the bed, she swore. "Where am I?"

"In your apartment, and if you don't hurry and get dressed..." the woman pointed at the slacks, "...you'll be late for work." She laid a blue blouse next to the pants. "Since you don't have time for a shower, I suggest you pull your hair up into a ponytail. If you hurry you'll make it just in time."

A loud racket started in the ceiling like a herd of buffalos tromping on the roof. "I told Ethan not to have the contractors start so early." Except this wasn't her home where he'd brought some of his workers in to install a light tube in her walk-in closet.

"Oh, that's just your neighbor." The woman pointed to the ceiling.

Janae scrambled to the far side of the bed and pulled the comforter up until only her eyes poked over the bedding. Her heart raced like someone had jolted it. This was not her luxurious home with its sweeping staircase, hardwood floors, and swimming pool.

Suddenly, she knew what this was about. "Oh, I get it. I'm on some sort of reality YouTube thingy, where there are hidden cameras, aren't I? Then it goes viral and everybody gets a good laugh." She'd watched enough of them to recognize a good joke.

Except, Ethan had never played pranks on her. Then who would do such a mean-spirited thing?

Her gaze drifted first to the kitchen area and then the closet at the foot of the bed, Janae couldn't find anything that looked like it might hold a camera, but that didn't mean they weren't there.

The woman popped a slice of bread into the toaster. "Nope, no reality show. This is the life you wished for."

"I've never wished for anything like this."

"You don't remember, do you?" The woman put her hands on her hips. Something about the gesture seemed so familiar.

Janae squinted her eyes. "I've seen you somewhere before: on the internet, TV, You Tube…maybe." She looked kind of like her mother's grandmother, Ana Bailey. That would explain the blond hair and blue eyes that was so predominant in her family. Though she'd never met her great-great grandmother, she'd heard enough stories and seen enough pictures to recognize her. "You're…you're…a ghost."

"Don't be silly. Ghosts can't pick things up and move them around. But an angel can."

Janae drew her eyebrows together. "What is an angel doing here?"

"Heaven thought you'd need someone to help you get your balance while you figure out things. So, they sent me." With a thumb, Ana gestured to herself.

Janae glared suspiciously at Ana. "Everyone in the family calls you Saint Ana." Although she suspected that it took a lot more than just being a good person to be called that.

If this wasn't reality television, this was the oddest and most real dream Janae had ever had. She pinched her arm. Ouch! She felt that.

She had to call Ethan and find out what was going on. A tattered, cheap purse that looked like it might have come from a thrift store sat on the nightstand. Who did that belong to? Certainly not Janae.

"And yes, that's your purse." Ana chuckled, a light twinkling in her eyes. "Oh, Saints are something completely different. Anyone can be a saint in Heaven, but angels…now that's a different story altogether."

"Really?" Janae didn't want to hear about the difference between the two ethereal beings, she just wanted to figure out what was on earth was happening to her.

Ignoring Ana, Janae searched through the contents of the purse and pulled out a phone that wasn't her iPhone. After examining it, she scrolled through the contacts. All of her family members were there. Why would someone go to such great lengths to prank her?

Ana reached across the bed and yanked the covers off Janae. "Now, get a move on if you want to be on time." She motioned to the clothes she'd laid out. "I'll explain everything on the way."

"On the way where?"

"Work, silly."

Okay, so Janae would just have to go along with this craziness until she could get to the bottom of her ordeal.

Janae stepped into the drab black slacks and tugged at a snag above the knee, hoping she didn't create a run. Did polyester do that? She'd never had a pair like these. The nondescript blue blouse fit her slender form. Someone knew her exact size and knew she hated collars.

After tying neon green tennis shoes, she grabbed the piece of toast and glass of orange juice Ana had fixed for her, Janae followed Ana out the door.

As Janae reached the end of the sidewalk, she turned to get a good look at where she supposedly lived. The two-story, four-plex with its chipped and peeling paint was not what Janae would have picked as her residence. If this horrible prank turned out to be Ethan's doing, she'd have more than just words for him. He could have chosen a posh apartment on the other side of town instead of this ramshackle building. They certainly had the money to afford a nicer place. Oh, but then this was a prank. It couldn't be Ethan, even though they'd had that horrible fight last night. He wouldn't have time to come up with something this complex. Yet, who else could she blame it on?

It took her a minute to locate the camera on the cheap phone before snapping a picture. This would be a hilarious post for her Instagram. *Husband plays cruel prank on his wife. Can you imagine me living here?* Okay, so maybe that was a bit of an exaggeration. Still...

Ana waved her to hurry. "Come on. You don't have time for that now."

Janae would have to upload it later. Her posts always got lots of like, comments and emojis when she shared her life.

Turning back to view the street, she recognized this neighborhood. Her husband's construction company was building a huge complex around the corner. "Not funny, Ethan, or whoever's scheme this is," she said into a flower bed. Somewhere in the dried-up mess there had to be a camera. She'd show them she could play along with their little game, and maybe later she and Ethan could laugh about it. It had been such a long time since they'd laughed about anything.

Janae bounced down the sidewalk and waved. She refused to give the film crew the satisfaction of surprise at anything that would happen to her today. She'd pretend she knew all about everything.

At the curb, she searched for her car, the Mercedes Ethan had purchased as an anniversary gift two years ago. Instead, she spotted an old, dilapidated Honda Accord, the same color as the one her daughter, Grace, drove. Passing by it, she turned to Ana. "How do I get to work? Does the light rail take me to the central offices? I'll bet I work as a paralegal for a law firm." It was what she'd done after she'd graduated college, and a short while after she married Ethan, to help put him through school.

Ana motioned to the Accord. "You're right about working downtown, but we're not riding the tram, we're taking your car."

"Oh, good. Anything is better than—" Janae turned to where Ana stood beside the beaten-up piece of junk. "You have got to be kidding me."

Ana pointed to Janae's purse. "Your keys are clipped to the side."

How had she missed the single key without a remote locking device when she'd searched her purse earlier?

Janae hesitated for a moment and then put the key in the car door. "This looks exactly like Grace's Honda…only older, much, much older." Oh, she was supposed to go along with this.

"This *was* Grace's car." Ana opened the passenger door and slid into the front seat. "Fortunately, your job is close by." Ana, or whoever the imposter was, pushed a stray piece of blond hair back in place.

Janae studied the woman for a moment. Whoever had planned this prank had done a wonderful job with the actress's makeup, making her look like the pictures Janae had seen in her mother's album. Ana couldn't really be an angel. She didn't believe in such nonsense.

The car turned over several times but wouldn't start. "Figures."

"It's been kind of finicky lately with the cold weather." Ana pointed to the ignition. "Try it again."

Grace never had trouble starting it. Ethan had made sure that it was always in good running condition.

"If you pump the gas a couple of times that should work."

With an eye roll, Janae played along and pressed the gas pedal a couple of times. This time it started and sputtered before settling into a stuttering idle. Someone with a remote starter probably helped it along.

Janae revved the engine. "All right, Ana, which way?"

"Head west toward Main and Central."

She put the car in drive and headed toward downtown.

When they passed the place where her husband's construction company was building the high-rise apartments, Janae slammed on her brakes. What she saw couldn't be right. The buildings were finished, and occupants clearly filled the apartments. A car behind her blared his horn, and Janae eased off the brakes. Setting her up in an apartment was one thing, but to build and fill this apartment complex overnight simply couldn't be done. Even on those reality shows houses took weeks to renovate.

Fear gripped her insides and snaked its way to her hands as she fought to find an explanation for this insanity. It was getting harder and harder to breathe. It just didn't add up. How could she have been sleeping next to Ethan last night and then wake up here the next? What was even happening?"

Ana rolled the window down, letting the brisk air drift across the front seat. She took a deep breath. "I just love the smell of winter."

Janae shivered. "Roll that up." Winter meant snow and wind, muddy shoes in the garage and laundry room, piles of boots by the back door. What would Christmas be like this year without Lili?

What in the world was she doing in a dilapidated car heading to work? Janae sat chewing her lip. Going along with this prank was ridiculous. As soon as she reached the next stoplight, she'd call Ethan and tell him she gave up.

As she drove down the street, trees and cars blurred at the edges of her vision. What would her husband say when she called him? What was his excuse? How long had he been planning this—and how far was he willing to go? It didn't make any sense. They'd fought before, but not bad enough for him to do something like this.

When the light turned red almost two blocks from downtown,

she reached into her purse, and pulled out her phone.

After scrolling through her contacts, she located Ethan's number, and hit the dial icon. After a couple of rings, the voice on the other end said, "We're sorry, the number you have dialed is no longer in service."

No longer in service? That was a little extreme for a prank. She dialed his office number.

"Williams Contracting." The voice on the other end did not sound like Claire, his secretary.

"This is Janae Williams; I need to speak to Ethan, immediately."

"I'm sorry, Ms. Bailey, Mr. Williams is on site and won't be available until late this afternoon." Her voice sounded clipped. "Can I get your number and have him call you later this afternoon?"

"He knows my number." Janae hung up. Bailey? Her maiden name? And why would he hire a new secretary? Did he fire Claire? She was perfect for the business. Janae had made sure she hired someone fresh out of college so that Ethan could train her the way he wanted and not have to correct the habits of a previous employer.

"A lot has changed in the last five years."

Janae jumped at the sound of Ana's voice. She'd almost forgotten her passenger.

This had gone too far. If the fight she'd had with Ethan last night was bad, just wait until she got home tonight.

Ana pointed to the stop light. "It's green, and if you don't step on it, you're going to be late for work."

Janae gripped the steering wheel. "What if I decide not to go to work?"

"If you don't, this will be the third job you've been fired from in the last two years."

"Two years?" The car behind her honked. Janae dropped her phone into her purse and sped through the light. "I live on 3695 E. Elm Place. I don't have a job. I've spent the last 17 years raising my children. I have three girls and one boy. My daughter died this summer in a drowning accident that would never have happened if my husband had been paying attention."

In a condescending tone, Ana said, "I hate to break it to you, but you've been divorced for almost five years. Grace is now a sophomore at the university. Taylor graduates from high school this year, and Ryan is playing on the varsity basketball team."

"And I suppose Ethan has remarried and moved on?" She hadn't meant to sound so sarcastic.

A look of sadness crossed Ana's face. "Actually, he's seeing someone, just casually, though."

"Who?" Janae asked, not believing that her husband would take his prank that far.

"Claire."

2

Trying to steady her breath, Janae pulled into the closest parking lot. A knife hit her stomach and twisted, stirring up the contents of breakfast slamming them against the bottom of her heart.

Claire?

Ethan would really strike up a relationship with a woman so much younger than him? Not that she was buying any of this anyway. Still it hurt that someone would have this actress person say such a thing.

To prove that this was a ridiculous set up, she pulled her wallet out. Her driver's license was the same, except…Bailey? That was her maiden name. Her debit card had the same name, Janae Bailey. That couldn't be right.

"I told you, you're divorced. You won't find your nail redemption card, your charge cards, or your signature perfume."

Ana was right. The nail salon card with six punches on it was nowhere to be found. A quick glance at her unmanicured hands confirmed what Ana had just said. Janae rummaged through her purse and all of her other items were missing. Okay, this was getting freakier by the minute. She pulled out a folded-up piece of paper. A paystub? Seriously, she only made slightly more than minimum wage working at…

Charity Dollar Store?

Examining it, she found no child deduction, making her take home a little over half of her gross. How did a person live on that? No wonder someone had made it looked like she lived in a studio apartment.

She'd put an end to this nightmare once and for all. She pulled out her phone and scrolled through her contacts again, stopping at Grace's.

Janae took a deep, steadying breath. Wasn't it just last night she'd questioned Grace about sneaking off to meet that boy? The phone rang a couple of times.

"Mom?"

Finally, someone who could tell her what was going on. "Hey, sweetheart. Would you come pick me up? I'm in a reality television show, and I'd like for it to end."

"Um, I'm on my way to Natalie's at the moment. I have to study for my final." After a long pause, Grace said. "Aren't you late for work?"

"Very funny, Grace." Janae tried to laugh. Her daughter must be in on the prank as well. "I'll write an excuse for you."

"Mom?" Her voice sounded so different. It was her daughter, but not quite. "You can't write notes to college professors."

"What is going on?" Her hands shook as she tried to hang onto the phone.

"I don't know what you mean. But if you lose this job, Dad's not going to help you out anymore."

"But…"

"I gotta go." Grace hung up.

Janae let the phone slide to her lap. "This isn't funny. Grace would never go along with this kind of joke."

"You're five years into the future. You've been divorced since February 13, 2015. Isn't that what you wanted?" Ana took Janae's hands and gently held them. "Isn't that what you wished for?"

Janae jerked her hands out of Ana's and gripped the steering wheel until her knuckles turned white. "What? I would never wish for something like this. Just take me home." Then maybe everything would make sense.

"I don't have the ability to do that. I'm limited to only serving as your advisor. Besides, you're the one driving."

Janae crossed her arms over the top of the steering wheel and rested her head on her elbows, her breakfast threatening to make an appearance. "Then what would you advise me to do?" She took in shallow breaths.

Ana rubbed her back. "Call your boss and tell him you're running late. Then get to work like you've done for the last three months."

This had to be one crazy dream, and hopefully she'd wake up soon. Janae turned the heater up, then scrolled through her contacts looking for…Charity Dollar?

Sheepishly, Janae stared at her phone. "I can't find the number."

With a shake of her head, Ana held out her hand.

Janae handed her phone to Ana.

She scrolled down to the bottom of her long list of contacts. "Right here under *work*."

Janae took the phone back and dialed.

A man answered whose accent was so thick, she could hardly understand him. "You late again. How you keep doing this to me?"

"I'm sorry, Mr. ..." Janae paused.

"Chang," Ana whispered.

"Right. Mr. Chang, I'm almost there." Janae winced. "I've had a horrible morning. I'll be there in a few minutes."

"This make twice this week." He hung up.

Ana smiled. "It's not as bad as it seems."

Janae turned to her passenger. "No, you're right; it's not as bad as…it's worse." Why in the world would she choose to work there of all places?

Ana pointed. "It's just up the block."

She knew where it was since she'd passed it several times when she'd gone downtown.

Once she reached Charity Dollar Store, she pulled into a parking space well away from the front door. This wasn't where she normally shopped, and yet something about this place seemed oddly familiar, even though she knew she'd never set foot inside. Janae loved the specialty shops and bigger department stores. Lately, she'd preferred online shopping. Dollar stores were for those with hardly any expendable income.

"Here you are." Ana smiled and then vanished.

Startled by Ana's sudden disappearance, Janae wrapped her arms around herself. "I have to be dreaming. People don't vanish like that. She clenched her teeth to steady her nerves, got out of the car, and trudged toward the strip mall avoiding the patch of ice between the parking spaces. Taking one last glance over her shoulder, she checked the car again for Ana. Nothing.

Without her angel to scold her, Janae was tempted to get back in the car and drive home...not the apartment home, but her spacious, two-story one on Elm Street.

"Don't even think about it." Ana's ethereal voice floated around her.

"I wasn't." Janae stomped the snow off her boots and opened the door to Charity Dollar.

Once she entered the store, stuffed with a sundry of cheap items, an Asian man met her, shaking a duster. "Long time I wait for you. You no see that we busy."

The least Janae could do was be polite. "Mr. Chang, I'm so sorry; it won't happen again."

Mr. Chang slammed his duster on the checkout counter. "No more late." With a wave of his bony hand, he left her standing at the front of the store. An indigent looking man turned his prying eyes back to the shelves.

It wasn't like Mr. Chang could have served his customers himself. She doubted, that besides the man examining the gloves on the rack, hardly anyone had been in yet today. Wait, what was she thinking? Like she was already familiar with her job? Hundreds of images poured into her mind as she remembered what she did all day, eleven to nine, four days a week. Who was taking care of the kids while she was working? Did they live with their father? She certainly didn't have room in her apartment for more than just herself.

What if this wasn't a prank for some YouTube video and this really was her new life? Had she been in some kind of accident that had messed with her brain and she was suffering from memory loss?

Surveying the disaster of disorganized shelves, dirty floors and boxes of items to be stocked, it would take someone months until the store was in any semblance of order. With a sudden realization, she put her palm to her head. She was only seasonal help, and she'd be out of a job after Christmas.

Maybe Mr. Chang would let her keep working if she proved

how invaluable she was. Janae stomped her foot. No, this all had to be some weird nightmare, and she'd wake up soon.

After stowing her purse in the back office, she turned to ask her boss what he wanted her to do, as if she didn't really know.

Mr. Chang sat at a desk. He had a phone perched between his shoulder and his ear, rattling to someone in his native tongue so fast that even if Janae spoke Chinese, she'd never be able to keep up with him.

Janae grabbed the blue apron with the company name embroidered across the front, and slipped it over her head, then tied the strings around her back. The bells on the front door jangled.

The first of a steady stream of customers entered the store. They wore worn out clothes, dragged snot-nosed children, and often counted their money in dimes and quarters to pay for their items. How could people live like this? Didn't anyone help them with Christmas gifts for their children?

By the time Mr. Chang's wife arrived, Janae was ready to turn the cash drawer over to her. Janae didn't know how she knew this was Mrs. Chang, but she did.

"You sell plenty?" She came around the back side of the cash register and opened the drawer, checked the number of bills, then ran a system scan of the register, verifying the total sales for the day. "Very good. Too bad you not stay after Christmas."

After her horrendously long day, Janae didn't care whether she stayed on after the holidays or not. All she wanted to do was get home and soak her aching feet in a hot tub. She couldn't even remember how she ended up working for the Changs in their abysmally cheap store. Why had she been reduced to such a menial job when she already had skills for a much higher paying one? At the very least, she could have been working for a higher end department store. On Monday, she would look for a better job.

Mr. Chang waved her out the door. "You be on time tomorrow."

The bitter cold blew around her. Janae wrapped her coat tighter around her body, pulled the scarf across her mouth, and ran to her car. The starter grinded as she turned the key in the ignition. Why wouldn't it start? What had Ana told her to do this morning? Janae pumped the gas a couple of times. Nothing she tried seemed to help.

Now how would she get home? If Grace was in college, she

probably had a car. Janae pulled out her phone.

"Hey sweetie, my car won't start. Can you come get me?"

"Mom, seriously. You know I have my play rehearsals until ten; I can pick you up around ten-thirty."

Janae had no idea her daughter was in a show, though she should have known. Theater had always been her thing in high school.

"Did you get the lead?" Janae asked, trying to keep her teeth from chattering.

"Oh my gosh, Mom." Her teenage angst was still intact. "Where have you been?"

That's what Janae wanted to know. The last five years were only now coming back to her in bits and pieces.

"I can't sit outside and wait for you. It's way too cold." Janae would freeze to death in that time.

"Call Taylor." Grace ended the conversation before Janae could chat with her.

Taylor had a car? Maybe that was one argument Ethan had won that she should be thankful for. Perhaps her husband's mother had put him up to it.

Janae hesitated for a moment before dialing her second oldest child.

"Hi, Mom." At least Taylor seemed happy to hear from her.

"Hey sugar, can you do your mother a huge favor."

"Sure, what is it?"

Janae breathed out a sigh of relief. "I'm stranded at work. Can you give me a ride home?"

"Oh, darn, I'm in Pine Bluff."

"What are you doing there?" Janae couldn't believe that Grace wouldn't know that her sister was out of town.

"Duh, hello…skiing trip."

"I'm sorry honey; it's been a long and very weird day. I guess I just forgot." Janae rubbed her fingers over her temple.

Silence filled the space between them for a moment. "There's a candlelight run in a bit. Call Grace."

"I already tried."

"How about Grandma?" The laughter of teens filled the other

14

end of the line. "I gotta go," Taylor said.

Several flakes of snow hit her windshield and stuck. *I can't call Ethan's mother, especially with the mess I'm in.* Mrs. Williams wasn't necessarily an unkind mother-in-law, but Janae never seemed to measure up. The kids were always a mess, the house a disaster. Every time Mrs. Williams started a sentence with, "If a person would just…," Janae knew who that person was. It had taken her years to finally feel like she measured up to Mrs. Williams's expectations, but even then…

Janae wished her own mother didn't live so far away. She couldn't stay here out in the cold, and no one else would come bail her out.

Janae bit her lower lip, and then dialed her ex mother-in-law. When was the last time they'd spoken? "Gina?"

"How nice of you to call." What did Janae sense in her mother-in-law's voice?

She hated calling Gina, but she just didn't see any other options. "I have a problem."

"Of course, you do." Was that frustration in her voice? Was she already in bed? Did Janae wake her up?

"My car won't start."

"Did you try pumping the gas pedal…?"

"Yes." This was typical of Mrs. Williams. Janae could never do anything right. "Grace is at rehearsal, and Taylor's in Pine Bluff."

"Are you at work?" Before Janae could answer, Mrs. Williams said, "Give me ten minutes. I'm already in my pajamas."

"I didn't wake you, did I?"

"No, Pops and I were just watching a television show." Gina said something in the background to Ethan's dad. "I'll be there in a few."

Janae wasn't sure if she felt relieved that her ex mother-in-law was coming to get her, or if she should have chanced taking the tram then walking home. It was only six blocks…through the snow…in the dark…in the worst neighborhood in town…What could be worse? Mrs. Williams or risk getting mugged?

3

Mrs. Williams pulled up alongside the broken-down car. Shivering, Janae jumped inside the warm SUV, glad she'd decided not to take the tram. "I'm sorry to drag you out at this time of the night. You're the best."

"I try." She swung out of the parking lot and headed east.

Janae waited for the tirade Mrs. Williams would blast at her because of whatever offense she'd done to lose Ethan. What if it wasn't Janae's fault at all? What if Ethan was having an affair with Claire all along, and Janae had found out about it.

She turned to face Mrs. Williams, afraid to ask, but had to know. "Gina, who do you blame for the divorce?"

Her snort of laughter caught Janae off guard. "It takes two to tango."

"I don't even know how to tango." She and Ethan had taken ballroom dancing lessons, at her mother-in-law's suggestion, but Janae never did master the tricky steps.

Gina kept her eyes on the road but answered. "You know what I meant."

Janae could remember parts of her life in the last five years, but didn't have any recollection of what had led up to the divorce. The last time she'd spoken to her husband had been an argument over Ryan. "Seriously, what happened with Ethan and me?"

Gina let out a huff. "That's what all of us wondered. Why would you leave a good man like him?"

"Good?" Janae balled her hands into fists around the strap on her purse. So like Gina to defend her son. "Did you know he's in a relationship with Claire?"

"Interesting."

That's all his mother could say? "Claire, his secretary. The one I thought I could trust."

"Ethan *is* a good man. If you let him go, it's only natural that someone would snatch him up. Since they already had a working relationship, it would be easy for them to—"

"Please, don't defend him just because he's your son." Janae released her hold on her purse and clasped her hands in her lap, the knuckles bulging. "He's been having an affair with her."

"That's ludicrous." Gina slammed on her breaks when the light turned yellow. "If you hadn't been so wrapped up in yourself, you would have realized what a great man you had."

Was Janae really that self-centered? She didn't think so. It was just like her mother-in-law to side with Ethan. She always did.

They sat in silence. Janae had no idea how to defend her actions; she couldn't even remember them.

When the light turned green, Gina eased into the intersection.

From the cross direction a truck barreled through the intersection slamming into the passenger side.

4

Five Years Earlier
December 12, 2014

Janae's head popped off her pillow. Shouldn't she be in pain with an accident like that? Feeling her face for bandages, her fingers ran over the smooth skin. No bumps or lacerations...nothing that indicated an accident. She hated when she napped during the day. It always left her disoriented and brought on strange dreams...

And yet, that was the strangest, most lifelike nightmare she'd ever had. Even when she had vivid pregnancy dreams, they did not rival what she'd experienced yesterday afternoon. She hadn't meant to fall asleep; too many tasks lay ahead of her. And why would she have called her mother-in-law to come to her rescue?

Yet, she couldn't shake the feeling that everything she'd experienced held an element of truth to it, like she'd slipped into an alternate life, one not quite belonging to Janae, but a life that was completely of her own making. She shook her head and rubbed the sleep from her eyes hoping to rid the dark cloud hanging over her.

Glancing over at the mug on the nightstand from her evening tea, she couldn't help that maybe Gina understood her better than she thought. The quote on the outside read, "Thanks for not selling my son to the band of gypsies wandering through. I raised him, but you're stuck with him." Janae chuckled and picked it up, then sipping the last of it she tucked it under her arm. Silly dream. Still, her mother-in-law's comments in her nightmare left her shaken and unsettled.

Remaking the bed, she glanced over at her pristine nightstand. She held out her phone and took a picture. Her great-grandmother's crocheted, lace doily made the perfect base for the vintage lamp, a couple of the small treasures handed down through the family from Ana. Her husband's dresser lay in complete disarray. She was sure Gina would have never allowed that when Ethan was growing up. Janae was tempted to post a side-by-side photo on Instagram. Why couldn't Ethan keep his side of the room tidy? She'd provided plenty of organizers: a basket for his papers, a pewter tray for his pocket contents, and a decorative Kleenex box. Papers and tissues strewn about declared the evidence that he didn't care about how their home looked.

If she posted what his half of the room looked like, she'd get tons of sympathy from other wives, but it would start yet another fight with Ethan. Ah, what the heck. She clicked *post* on the two photos with a caption that read: *Anyone else have this battle?*

Janae loved the look of her immaculate bedroom, the one room in the house where she had once found peace, the one where she had enjoyed the company of her husband. Now it had become a war zone, along with every other room in the house.

Janae sat on the edge of the bed and picked up her pillow and plumped it. She brought it to her chest and hugged it close to her. Liliana had been about this big. With Janae's face pressed into the pillow, her tears darkened the lavender fabric. If only this was her darling little girl, but instead it was a pillow... if only she could hold Liliana once more. If only she could keep her safe. She would've done anything to feel her daughter's heartbeat softly against her chest.

Grace tapped on the doorframe. "I'm going to Natalie's to study."

Janae set the pillow back in place, smoothing the case, then looked up at Grace. Her sixteen-year-old daughter held a notebook to her chest. Scowling, Janae said, "That's an awful lot of make-up for studying." She also noted the shirt Grace wore wasn't the one she'd come home from school in. This one showed a little more cleavage than Janae was comfortable with.

Shrugging, Grace slid the notebook higher up her chest until it reached her chin. "I just felt kind of ugly when I got home."

"Uh-huh. When do you worry about your looks around Natalie?"

"So, can I go or not?"

Janae suspected this had to do with that boy. "Will Dylan be there?"

A soft huff escape Grace. "No, Mom, he will not be there."

"I don't like you hanging out with him."

Before Janae could list her reasons yet again, Grace tapped on the edge of her notebook. "He's a nice guy. He doesn't drink or smoke or do drugs. He gets really good grades…"

Janae glanced at the scar on Grace's arm where that other supposed boyfriend pushed her off the trampoline. "And you're still much too young for a boyfriend."

A whine edged Grace's voice. "Mom…"

"Grace, and I mean it." Some things Janae would not budge on. "I'll take you to Natalie's."

"I can take my car. You do remember that Dad let me have Grandma's."

Another source of irritation with her husband. Was he trying so desperately to assuage his guilt over Lili's death by letting Gina give Grace her old Honda?

A sixteen-year-old had no business owning a car. It gave her too much freedom for things that might get her into trouble. But what could Janae do? Ethan had agreed with his mother to take the car, just like he hadn't consulted with Janae about paying for summer basketball camp for Ryan and art classes for Taylor.

With resignation, Janae answered, "All right, but call me when you get there and before you come home, so I can watch for you. It's supposed to get really cold tonight; take a jacket."

"Okay. Thanks, Mom." Grace backed out of the doorway as if Janae might change her mind.

"I never had a car when I was in high school." Janae would call Grace later, to make sure her daughter was where she said she'd be.

Janae went back to smoothing the pillowcase. If only her problems disappeared as easily. She let the tears flow again. Ethan had barely shed any for Lili. The only time she'd seen him show any emotion was that one time he sat on the edge of his daughter's bed, holding a stuffed animal. As soon as he looked up and saw her watching him, he set the elephant against the pillow, pushed past her, and left the room.

Janae wiped the tears from her eyes. She'd shed enough tears for Ethan to drown in... just like Lili.

Her gaze shifted back to his dresser. Why had she even bothered to set up the document reader at his office? He still insisted on bringing half of it home with him.

He didn't seem to care that she cooked for him, cleaned for him, even met his physical needs. Would it hurt for him to keep his dresser top organized? Or at the very least, empty his pockets in the den?

The front door closed. There he was now. She'd have to have a chat with him about more than his dresser top.

Janae took the stairs at a slow pace, clenching and unclenching her fists.

Ethan took off his coat and laid it on the arm of the couch. Two feet, that's all he had to walk to hang up his jacket in the coat closet. Did he have no consideration for how hard she worked to keep their home beautiful enough to impress even his mother?

Grace bounded back through the front door. "I almost forgot my notes." She ran into her room and came back flailing a handful of papers.

"Off to study?" Ethan asked.

"Yep." Grace kissed him on the cheek and headed out the door. "Bye, Dad."

"I'll call you in a bit," Janae hollered after her.

Without a backward glance, Grace flung her hand in the air and practically skipped down the sidewalk. If any of the neighbors looked on, they'd think the Williams were a model family. Three perfect children, a beautiful, spacious home in one of the upscale neighborhoods. Ethan owned a thriving construction business, allowing Janae to be the contented stay-at-home mother.

That was before this summer.

Liliana was gone, and everyday Ethan grew more distant.

When she turned back around, he'd left the living room and headed up the stairs.

Snatching the coat off the couch, she went to the closet and yanked a hanger from the rod. She hung up his jacket, and followed him, bracing herself for the next battle.

Instead of heading into their bedroom, Ethan went into his den.

Janae stood in the doorway, contemplating the war in his domain. "Ethan, we need to talk about Ryan's grades."

Ethan threw his business folder on his desk, a flutter of papers dissipated like leaves from a blower. He slumped down in his chair and turned to face her. "Is he getting kicked off the basketball team?"

"Basketball season doesn't start until after Christmas. However, his teacher called this afternoon, and he's missing six assignments. The end of the semester is—"

"I'm sure he'll get them in before—"

"Don't defend him." This is how their discussions always went. He never listened to her.

Ethan opened his folder and pulled invoices out, then turned on his computer. "We'll talk to him at dinner."

"He's spending the night at the Henderson's after practice."

Setting the invoices aside, he swiveled his chair back around. "If you're so concerned about his grades, then why didn't you insist that he come straight home and work on his assignments?"

Oh, sure, throw it back on her. Why did she always have to be the disciplinarian? "Just once, could you back me up here?"

"You're the one who is at home all day; you're the one who the kids ask for these extra favors, when they *should* be doing more important things."

Janae clenched her jaw. "Only because you're never home. He's your son, too."

Ethan stood, forcing his chair backward. It slammed against the wall. "I work all day."

"And I don't? You think I just sit around the house and watch cat videos all day?"

Raking his hands through his hair, he stepped toward her. "That's not what I meant, and you know it."

Janae punched her hands on her hips. "Then what did you mean?"

He paced the small office space. "You could have checked his grades at any time before school got out. You're not lacking in tech savvy." He motioned to the phone clutched in her hand. "You could have told him that you needed to check his grades first before letting him go to his friend's house. You could have just said no at any point."

"Well, I didn't check them until after I'd already said yes." She took a step back.

Ethan had never hit her before, but the look in his eye said he just might, especially when he took an aggressive step toward her. "You're the one who said yes, so you deal with it."

"Just like I do everything else," she muttered under her breath and left the room.

5

Dinner was a silent affair. Ethan had taken his plate of food upstairs, claiming he had a lot of paperwork to do. What did they hire a secretary for anyway?

Taylor plowed through her meal and raced to her room to watch art videos. Alone at the table, Janae swiped through her phone, avoiding the call to Ryan telling him he needed to come home. No sense in completely ruining his evening with his friend.

Instead, she called Grace. It went straight to voicemail. Janae pursed her lips together. That girl had been boy-crazy since second grade. At least she hadn't let it affect her schoolwork. Still, Dylan was her latest crush. He might be nice enough, but Janae knew boys and what they wanted. Their hormones controlled every thought in their head.

She dialed Natalie's phone. "Hey, I need to talk to Grace."

Silence on the other end sent warning bells off in Janae's head.

"Oh, she went to the corner market to get some sodas. I'll tell her you called as soon as she gets back." Natalie's excuse didn't sound convincing.

Did she dare tell Ethan their daughter was probably out with that boy? Her husband would blow it off, like chasing after a young man at sixteen was natural.

Okay, so it was normal. But lying about it and sneaking off with him went against everything Janae was trying to teach her children.

A few minutes later Grace called. "Hey, what's up?"

"Why did you shut your phone off?" Janae and Ethan had specifically purchased phones for their children so they could get ahold of them.

"Sorry, Mom," Grace said. "My phone was dead, so I left it at Natalie's house so it could charge."

"Where did you go that you needed to leave your phone behind?" Janae was going to make Grace admit she'd been with that boy.

"Uh, to the store to get some more sodas."

"Was that boy with you?"

"His name is Dylan. And no, he was not."

Janae wasn't sure she believed her. "Be home by ten."

"But we're not done."

"You still have time before your assignment's due." Janae didn't wait for her daughter to reply. Next, she dialed Ryan. "I know I said you could spend the night, but Dad and I talked about your grades. We think it's a good idea if you come home."

"Seriously? You said, 'yes' before."

"I know but that was *before* we saw your grades."

"Mom…" That familiar whine came through the phone.

"You'll have other times…"

"What does it matter right now? I can't turn anything in on Saturday."

"Ryan Buckley Williams, I'm not having this argument with you right now. When you get your assignment turned in, then you can spend the night at Preston's."

"They're all done."

"Did you hand them in?"

"Some of them. She just hasn't graded them yet."

"That's good." Janae wondered if he was feeding her a line. "When they all get graded, I'll reconsider you spending the night. I'll be there to pick you up in about ten minutes." Again, she hung up before he could protest.

She grabbed her keys, pressed auto start on her Mercedes and drove the short distance to the Henderson's home. Then, after dragging her son home, Janae went into the family room and curled up on the leather couch, opened the YouTube app on her phone, and watched cat videos until Grace was due home. She needed to distract her mind from the constant worries that threatened to explode, as if time was always against her. She thought of that strange dream, where her greatgrandmother had come to her. Dreams had meaning. So, what did this one mean? With a sigh she glanced at the photo of her and Ethan on their wedding day. Mom had hand-stitched the lace to her veil. A twinge of a smile didn't match the large one on her face in the picture. Too much had happened since that day.

Her eyes drifted to each of the framed school pictures of her children. Even Lili's candid picture sat on the cabinet with her older siblings. As Janae imagined Lili's kindergarten picture along with the others, tears prickled.

With the back of her hand, Janae swiped the moisture away and went back to her phone where memories didn't haunt her.

A few moments later, keys jangled in the front door. Janae didn't look up from her phone when Grace entered the room but noted the time. Right on curfew. "Did you get your project finished?" Janae took a quick glance at her daughter.

Grace kept her coat on and held her notebook like a shield. "Almost."

"Will you have it ready to turn in by next Tuesday?" Janae wished Ryan was more like his older sister, always on top of her schoolwork, except when she wasn't thinking about the male gender. She set her phone down and eyed Grace. "You're sure about not hanging out with that boy?"

Grace rolled her eyes. "I told you he wasn't going to Natalie's."

"Did you meet him at the store when you went for soda?"

"Oh my gosh, I didn't hang out with Dylan tonight."

"You've never lied to me before."

"And I'm not lying now." Grace clutched the notebook tighter.

"All right, then." Janae longed for the times when her oldest daughter would sit on her bed and they'd cuddle as Grace would tell her mother everything. Had all that changed because Lili died, or was it because Grace was growing up? Janae eyed her oldest daughter a moment longer. "Don't stay up too late."

"It's Friday!" Grace left the room.

By the time Janae was ready for bed, all three of her children were accounted for—Ryan angry at having to come home, the other two hidden in their rooms. Janae suspected they didn't want to listen to their parents arguing. She didn't blame them and often wanted to hide as well.

She poked her head into Grace's room.

Grace sat with her face in her phone…texting that boy, probably.

Janae twitched her mouth to the side, watching her oldest daughter. "Dylan?"

Grace rolled her eyes. "We're just friends!"

"Good, keep it that way."

The light was off in Taylor's room. Her fourteen-year-old lay still under her blankets. "Good night," Janae whispered in the dark.

"Mom?" Taylor whispered back.

Janae entered the room. "Yeah, sweetie, what is it?"

Her voice had a quiet resignation to it. "Are you and Dad getting divorced?"

Sitting on the edge of the bed, Janae stroked the hair off Taylor's forehead and tucked it behind her ear. "Why would you say that?"

She rolled onto her back. "You and dad just seem to fight all the time. Nobody in this house is happy anymore."

With a small shake of her head, Janae dropped her hands in her lap. "Sometimes adults just have to work things out."

"I guess." Taylor curled onto her side facing the wall. "Beth's parents don't fight, ever."

"I'm sure they do, but not where anyone can see."

Taylor shrugged. "But they're so happy all the time."

They might seem that way, but Janae sensed some couples were just better at hiding their marital problems behind closed doors. "Looks can be deceiving." She patted Taylor's shoulder. "Sweet dreams."

Taylor didn't answer.

Janae stood watching her daughter's breathing settle as she drifted off to sleep. Wouldn't it be nice to forget her troubles that fast?

Ryan's door was closed. Janae knocked softly before cracking it open. The room was pitch black and she had a hard time making out the lump in his bed. "G'night Ryan," she whispered, wishing he hadn't been so angry when she'd brought him home. He hadn't even eaten the dinner she'd put in the microwave. Hopefully the Hendersons had fed him.

Ethan probably didn't even realize Ryan had come home.

"Good night, Ryan," Janae said a little louder.

He didn't answer. Maybe she could take him out for an ice cream tomorrow and talk to him about his grades. It wasn't like basketball was a huge deal this year. The boys only played other teams in the same school. Next year when he got into junior high things would be different. She hoped by then he'd develop better study habits.

Out of routine, Janae stopped by Lili's room and flipped on the light. For a brief moment, she expected to find her five-year-old tucked in her bed, her clothes strewn across the floor, and a number of stuffed animals piled along the side of her bed, like a small army marshaled in ranks, smallest to largest.

With no messes on the floor, the neatness of it all stabbed at Janae's heart. She wished her mother-in-law had left it a mess. Gina had probably thought she was trying to help, but Janae wanted to desperately scold Lili one more time to pick up after herself. It would mean her youngest daughter was alive.

When would Janae ever get used to not having Lili? Could she ever forgive Ethan?

Janae couldn't bring herself to enter Lili's room. Instead, she turned off the light and walked down the long hall to her bedroom. The time on her phone said 10:22. Too early to go to bed, too late to start a movie.

More and more often, Janae avoided going to bed until Ethan's soft snores filled the room. She hated his snoring; it made it hard for her to fall asleep, but tonight she didn't want him keeping her awake while she struggled with her inner turmoil. He no longer understood her and what she went through every day, thinking about how empty the house was without her youngest daughter. How could God have taken her precious daughter away after having a still-born baby? Not that Liliana would ever replace the little boy, but Lili was her hope for a brighter tomorrow.

Lili was supposed to have started school this fall. "When do I get to meet my teacher?" she had asked when Janae took Ryan to his classroom to meet his sixth-grade teacher.

"Next year." Janae held onto Lili's hand.

Lili stomped her foot, her blond curls bouncing at the gesture. "That's too long!"

Janae had laughed and ruffled Lili's hair...so different than Taylor and Ryan's who both favored their father's dark chocolate colored hair. "How about going to preschool?"

Lili dragged her feet. "That's not a real school."

On the day school started, Janae had tried to console Lili by taking her to the movies. Truth be told, Janae was looking forward to the next year when she'd have the whole day to herself. For now, she had told herself to be content that she would have a couple of days a week to work on her projects while her youngest headed off to preschool. Now Janae would give just about anything to spend all day with Lili.

Without turning on her bedroom lights, she shed her clothes, crawled into bed. Ethan's soft snores filled the quiet room. She'd poke him later and get him to roll over. In the meantime, she opened her IG app and checked how many likes she got on her post before scrolling through the comments.

I feel your pain.

Looks like my dresser. The hubs is always complaining.

Scoop it into a box and hide it in the closet.

A least he's working hard for the family.

She responded:

I work hard, too.

When her phone indicated she was down to 15%, she plugged it in and snuggled against her pillow.

Ethan rolled toward her and placed his heavy hand on her neck and stroked her hair. She cringed. How could he go from yelling at her one moment to wanting self-gratification the next?

Janae wriggled out from under his touch and scooted closer to the edge of the king-size bed. Once again, she found herself sleeping on the binding. Taylor's words echoed in her mind. *Are you and Dad getting divorced?*

She let out a soft huff. "I wish I *was* divorced," she whispered into the air.

6

Friday, Dec 13, 2019

Someone tapped her on the foot. "Wake up, sunshine, or you're going to be late! You only have thirty minutes to get ready. I'll make some toast."

Janae rolled over and eyed Ana as she stood beside the bed looking exactly as she had the last time. Why was she repeating the same nightmare? "I don't have a job."

"Oh, but you do." The woman pulled a pair of black slacks out of a tiny closet near the foot of the bed and draped them on the end.

How odd that she should have the same dream two nights in a row. "Why am I back here?"

The woman didn't answer her. She laid a blue blouse next to the pants. "If you hurry, you'll make it just in time."

"In time for what?"

The same loud racket started in the ceiling, like a herd of buffalos tromping on the roof.

Janae flung her legs over the side of the bed. "What are they doing up there?"

"Dancing." Ana pointed to the ugly clothes at the end of the bed. "Hurry up."

If this wasn't a reality show with hidden cameras, what was this? Why was she dreaming the exact same thing all over? Did she look for cameras she wouldn't find? Could she pinch herself awake? Janae grabbed the skin on the back of her arm and squeezed. "Ouch!"

Ana chuckled. "It's real. *This* is real. This is your life now. The one you wished for."

"I never wished for anything like this." Janae squinted her eyes at the same room as her last dream.

Ana put the toast on a plastic plate, then went to the miniature refrigerator and took out a small bottle of juice and poured a glass. "Get a move on if you want to be on time."

"On time for what?"

"Your job, silly girl!" Ana motioned to the clothes she'd laid out. "I'll explain everything on the way to work."

Just like the last time, Janae dressed and grabbed the toast and juice Ana had fixed for her, and then they headed out the door.

As Janae reached the end of the sidewalk, she turned to get a good look at where she *lived*. Sure enough, it was the same one she'd snapped a picture of yesterday. Like she'd done in her previous dream, she pulled out her phone and took the same photo and posted it in her Instagram account. *Ever have déjà vu? Me, too. This morning's weirdness brought to you by a mini seizure or a horrible nightmare.* This next part of her bad dream would be trying to start the car.

Pumping the gas brought the Honda to life. "See, I remember what you told me yesterday."

Ana had slipped into the passenger side. "Yesterday? Are you sure?"

Janae studied the woman for a moment. "Let me guess, I work at Charity Dollar as a salesclerk, and I'm only seasonal. By the end of December, I'll be jobless, yet again."

"Wonderful. You remembered!" Ana clapped her hands as if Janae had performed some major feat. "Head west on Main."

She put the car in drive and headed toward downtown.

When they passed the place where her husband's construction company was building the high-rise apartments, Janae slowed down. The same edifice filled with occupants still sat on the corner.

Ana rolled the window down, letting the brisk air drift across the front seat, and took a deep breath. "I just love the smell of winter."

Janae shivered. "Roll that up."

Winter meant snow and wind, muddy shoes in the garage and laundry room; piles of boots by the back door…Ethan's coat on the arm of the chair in the living room. She frowned at the memory of hanging it up where it belonged. Her thoughts even repeated themselves like they had in her previous nightmare. She couldn't help the next thought. What would Christmas be like this year without Lili?

No, she wouldn't think about yesterday. She'd think about the personalized gifts she'd purchased for each of her children. For Grace, she bought a hand-blown glass rabbit. A habit rabbit, she'd called it. That was Grace, always thinking of ways to better herself. Taylor wanted jewelry, a moon-phase necklace specific to her birthday. For Ryan, she'd splurged on a wooden box shaped like a guitar. Inside it nestled three engraved guitar picks. The first one said, *Couldn't pick a better son*, the second had a picture of his favorite guitarist, and the third— *Strum your way to happiness*. The box hung on a chain to go around his neck.

For Lili, she bought a pink backpack just her size and filled it with all the things she loved: a pair of unicorn shoes, a box of crayons with a coloring book, and a music box that played *The Wheels on the Bus*. Janae planned to donate the backpack in Lili's memory to the school for some child who might need it.

She shook herself out of her thoughts. How in the world did she end up back in this freaky dream?

When the light turned red almost two blocks from downtown, she reached into her purse, the same tattered, cheap one she'd had in her last dream. Janae had always been good with details, so then why couldn't she have dreamed about her iPhone nestled inside her Givenchy handbag?

She went through the contacts and located Ethan's number, then hit the dial icon. After a couple of rings, the voice on the other end said, "We're sorry, the number you have dialed is no longer in service."

No longer in service? Oh, that's right, he'd changed his number. She dialed the company office.

"Williams Contracting." The voice on the other end did not sound like Claire.

"This is Janae Williams; I need to speak to Ethan, immediately."

"I'm sorry, Ms. Bailey, Mr. Williams is on site and won't be available until late this afternoon." The secretary had the same clipped tone as the last time. "Can I get your number and have him call you later this afternoon?"

Janae hung up. Bailey? Outside her dream she was certain of her name—Williams, not Bailey. And why would he hire a new secretary? Oh, that's right, Ethan was off having his little fling with Claire.

"The light turned green and if you don't step on it, you're going to be late for work," Ana said.

Janae jumped at the sound of Ana's voice. Once more, she'd almost forgotten her passenger.

7

Janae couldn't wait to wake up from this horrid nightmare. She pulled into a parking space close to the front doors of Charity Dollar. Nope, nothing had changed here either. The store front sported the same cheap decorations and cheesy window paintings that a six-year-old could have done.

Janae picked up her phone and dialed Grace.

"Mom?" Her voice sounded as surprised as she had in her last dream. "What's going on?"

"I need you to talk some sanity into me." Janae tried to force a chuckle, but it came out rough like she was holding back a cough.

"You haven't been sane since Lili died." Grace's words cut her to the core.

"What year is it?"

"Really?" Grace blew out a huff that carried as if she'd blown it straight into Janae's ear. "I've got to go."

Ana's soft hands took Janae's and gently held them. The gesture familiar in some way that Janae couldn't pinpoint. Maybe a hereditary thing. "You're five years into the future. You've been divorced for almost that long. Isn't this what you wished for?"

Janae jerked her hands out of Ana's and gripped the steering wheel until her knuckles turned white. "Well let's see what the rest of this nightmare is like." Janae got out of the car and headed toward her place of employment.

Hopefully, she'd wake up soon.

Once she entered the front door, she eyed the shelves stuffed with a sundry of cheap items. Mr. Chang shook his feather duster at her. "Long time I wait for you! You no see we busy!"

Janae didn't answer but took another look around at the interior.

He slammed his duster on the checkout counter. "No more late!" With a wave of his bony hand, he left her standing at the front of the store. An indigent man turned his prying eyes back to the shelves.

The same memories flooded her mind. What if this wasn't a dream or a prank? Maybe she had been in some kind of accident that had messed with her brain, and she was suffering from memory loss…and this was her life. What if this really was her life?

Gingerly touching her head, she felt for any scars that might explain why her memories were sketchy but felt nothing. Then again, head injuries didn't often result in visible wounds.

In the back office, her boss sat at his desk with a phone to his ear, rattling to someone in his native tongue.

Janae examined the apron before slipping it over her head, a plain blue with the company logo on the front.

The bells on the front door jangled, and Mr. Chang waved her out of the office.

The same customers as the last time entered the store. They wore the same worn-out clothes, dragging their same snot-nosed children, and continued to count their money in the same dimes and quarters.

After her long day, Mr. Chang's wife entered. "You sell plenty?" She came around the back side of the cash register and opened the drawer, checked the number of bills, then ran a system scan of the register, verifying the total sales for the day. "Velly good. Too bad you not stay after Christmas." Everything about her dream was exactly the same, even down to how exhausted she felt. Her back ached, her feet hurt, and a jackhammer pounded in her head. All she wanted to do was to go home, fall into bed and wake up tomorrow back in her home.

Mr. Chang opened the door for Janae. "You be on time tomorrow."

Janae waved at him then went out into the bitter cold. The starter grinded when she turned the key in the ignition. *Oh, that's right, pump the gas pedal.*

It still didn't start. Grace was at rehearsal; Taylor was in Pine Bluff.

Several flakes of snow hit her windshield and stuck. She couldn't stay out here in the cold.

Janae bit her lower lip, and then dialed just like she'd done the last time. "Gina?"

"How nice of you to call." Her mother-in-law said. Nothing in her voice had changed.

"My car won't start."

"Did you try pumping the gas pedal…"

"I did. Grace is at rehearsal and Taylor's in Pine Bluff on a ski trip. I'm at work…would you mind?"

"Give me ten minutes. I'm already in my pajamas."

8

Gina pulled up alongside Janae's broken-down car. Shouldn't there have been some damage after the accident? Shivering, Janae jumped inside the warm SUV. "I'm sorry to drag you out into the cold for the second night in a row."

"Second?" Gina swung out of the parking lot and headed east.

Oh, that's right. This was a repeat of the day before and there wouldn't be any damage to her car. "Never mind." She turned to face her mother-in-law. "What happened with Ethan and me?"

Gina let out a huff. "That's what all of us wondered. Why would you leave a good man like him?"

Janae balled her hands into fists around the strap on her purse. "Did you know he's in a relationship with Claire?"

"Interesting."

In her last nightmare Janae had told her about Ethan and Claire.

Gina slammed on her breaks when the light turned yellow.

They sat in silence.

The light turned green and Gina eased into the intersection. From the cross direction a truck barreled through the intersection slamming into the passenger side.

9

Thursday, Oct 31, 2013

Janae kept her eyes closed. She expected to be in a hospital bed. She felt for pain in her limbs and gingerly touched her head. That truck had been coming too fast. Maybe she was dead and that's why nothing hurt. Or maybe it was all just part of the same nightmare. She'd wake up and find herself back in her bedroom. Did she dare peek?

"Mama, I'm hungry."

Lili? Janae's eyes flew open and her five-year-old daughter stood in front of her. How could that be? Lili was dead. She'd felt the smoothness of the casket under her fingertip, remembered Ethan's voice trying to soothe her. But here she was looking into Lili's face. That must mean…

Janae sat up. She *was* back in her bedroom and Lili…she was alive! Her heart danced with joy. Wait, what if Janae had died, then were they both in Heaven? Then death wasn't so bad after all. With outstretched arms, she gathered Lili onto her lap, rolled her over, and tickled her neck with her lips.

Giggling, Lili said, "I want some skwambled eggs wiff little pieces of bacon."

"Then that is what I shall make for you." Did people eat food in the afterlife? She didn't care. She had her Lili and that was all that mattered.

Ethan walked into the room, in jeans, a pocketed t-shirt and his work boots. "Are you going to sleep all day?"

Janae glanced at the clock. "It's only seven."

"I'm just teasing. Sleep as long as you want." He smiled and his face brightened, crinkling the lines next to his blue eyes. This was the man she'd fallen in love with eons ago when they met at college. "Don't forget the repairman is coming over this morning to check on the pool pump." He studied them for a moment. Did he not realize Lili was alive? How could that be when she'd drowned last summer?

Upon closer examination, Lili looked about three years old, down to her cute little way of pronouncing her words, not the five-year-old child she'd lost.

Tears of joy ran down Janae's cheeks. "Oh, baby, I've missed you so much."

Lili pointed to herself. "Silly Mommy, I wight here."

"Yes, you are!" She hugged her tight against her chest, letting the tears flow unabashed.

Ethan shook his head. "You're so emotional, are you expecting a visit?"

Janae ignored his comment. "Let's get you some breakfast." She set her daughter on the floor and they left the bedroom with Lili's hand gripped in hers.

Taylor sat at the breakfast bar drinking a glass of juice. If Lili was three, that made her middle daughter twelve. She wore her favorite pink flowered pants with a t-shirt that barely matched. How her style would change in three short years. For now, Janae reveled in her daughter's innocence.

After a large gulp, Taylor asked, "Beth is having a sleep over tonight after the party, can I go?"

Janae tried to remember back to that night, except she had no idea which sleepover. It could have been any time of the year. The last time she'd let Ryan spend the night without checking his grades first, Ethan had blown up at her. That was a different time after Lili drowned. Still. "Um…let me think about it."

"Mom…" Taylor whined.

Janae's nerves grated at her daughter's tone. She went to the kitchen window and stared out at the backyard. The trees were bare, so it must be fall. The party had to be the one Beth's family threw every year for Halloween.

Nothing bad had happened, so it might be alright. "I suppose." Still something niggled at her memory. Wait! Something *had* happened that night. What was it?

Then it dawned on her, it wasn't Taylor who'd get hurt; it was Grace. She remembered it as clearly as if she'd been living it. She *was* living it.

If she let Taylor go, she'd have to let Grace go to her party as well, and that would mean a trip to the ER and months in a cast. Maybe this was her chance to rectify the past and save her daughters.

Lili climbed onto the barstool next to Taylor. "I come, too?"

Taylor rolled her eyes. "No babies allowed."

Janae cringed. If Taylor knew that in two short years her sister might be dead, she wouldn't be speaking like that. Life was too precious. Yet, she couldn't scold Taylor for something she didn't know would happen.

Lili held up her fingers. "I not a baby. I fwee years old."

Janae ran her finger down her youngest daughter's nose. "You are getting so big, but this party is for older kids."

"I wanna go." Lili flopped onto the counter and wailed.

Janae hated her tantrums. She had to stop it now before she got out of hand. For all her cuteness, Lili already had an attitude that would certainly give her trouble once she hit her teenage years, if Janae had a hand in changing the past.

"I have a better idea." She picked up Lili and slung her over her shoulder and tickled her sides. "Grace and Taylor can take you trick-or-treating instead of Daddy. Would you like that?"

Taylor rolled her eyes. "Mom." She dragged Janae's name out. "It's Beth's one and only Halloween party of the year."

Ethan stood in the doorway between the kitchen and dining room. "I was planning on taking Lili trick-or-treating."

Janae set Lili back on the barstool and stared at him for a few moments, trying to figure out how best to handle the situation. She couldn't just tell him she was from the future and knew what was going to happen to Grace and later Liliana. He'd think she was a lunatic. "Well, maybe the three of you could go together."

Ethan entered the kitchen, wrapped his arms around her waist, and kissed her. "Or maybe we can turn off all the lights and disappear for the evening. I'm sure Grace can handle taking the kids."

Part of her melted against him. She couldn't remember the last time he'd kissed her like this. Why were her toes curling at his touch and her stomach fluttering like they were dating? She had to remember Lili's death was his fault.

But Lili was alive. Janae could fix it and go on loving Ethan as she had before, couldn't she?

Ryan pushed his way into the kitchen. His disheveled hair stood on end. That would quickly change once he entered junior high. "Ew, gross, get a room, already." He opened the refrigerator and pulled out the milk.

"Ew, gwoss, get a woom alweady."

Ethan chuckled. "Don't say anything you don't want her to repeat." He released Janae. "We have a room, in fact a whole house. And if you'd like to pay the mortgage, then you can dictate where I get to kiss your mother."

Grace entered the room and sat next to Taylor, picked up the carton, and poured herself a glass of orange juice. Not much had changed with Janae's oldest daughter. Her blond hair lay in curls over her shoulder. "I think it's sweet. I hope my husband isn't ashamed to kiss me any time he wants."

Janae cleared her throat and looked into Ethan's blue eyes, loving that he still loved her in this moment. These were the good times she remembered. When had her marriage gone so bad? Oh, yeah. After Lili died. How could she stop that from happening?

10

Taylor grumped around the house all afternoon, mumbling her irritation under her breath, but loud enough that Janae heard every word. She had probably conspired with Grace to make Janae doubt her decision for the kids to all stay together tonight. Luckily, Ryan hadn't objected. He probably liked the idea of embarrassing his older sisters.

The sad thing about the girls taking Lili out trick-or-treating was that Grace would never thank her mother for not going to the ER. Janae would do everything she could to protect her children, even if it meant Grace would hate her for the rest of her life. It didn't matter. Janae was doing the right thing.

"Hold still, my little rug rat." Janae set Lili on the bathroom counter.

"I want a gween nose wiff a wart, and scary ghost eyes."

Janae wished her daughter preferred fairies and princesses. Then again, Lili never liked what most little girls did. She loved trucks and ghosts and scary monsters.

"You can have whatever you want." Janae dabbed the green makeup over Lili's face.

Ethan crowded into the downstairs bathroom with them. "Oh, look at my scary goblin!"

Lili put her hands on her hips in the way that always made Janae laugh. "I not a goblin, I a witch." Her lip poked out in an adorable pout.

Ethan patted her tummy. "Oh, sorry, Griselda."

She folded her arms and turned her nose into the air. "I going to get lots of candy."

"I'm sure you will." He nuzzled his chin against the back of Janae's neck. "I might get some, too."

Suddenly the room grew ten times smaller, and with Ethan's cologne wafting around her, it made it as many times harder for Janae to think. "Okay, Mr. Stud-muffin, you go stand over there." She pointed to the hall. Janae hadn't called him that in eons.

With a look of mock rejection, Ethan left the bathroom, but stood outside, leaning on the door jam, that obvious look of man-hunger written all over his face. When was the last time they'd enjoyed each other's company? A lot before they lost Lili. Could she forgive him for their daughter's death when she was right here? Could she warn him of the impending doom?

Maybe she'd been sent back to this time to correct the mistake.

Lili bundled into her jacket before Janae slipped the witch costume over her head.

"Okay, hold still." Janae held up her phone to capture this moment. She could hardly wait to post it to all her social media accounts to show how clever she'd been in creating costumes they could wear over their coats.

As Ethan stood with Janae at the door, watching their little brood head off down the street, Ethan wrapped his arms around Janae's waist. "So, Mrs. Williams…"

How could she think when he was so near her? "Hold on." She wiggled out of his grip and clicked on the link to take her to her *if-this-then-that* app so it would post simultaneously to all her social media accounts.

He wrestled her iPhone from her hands and wrapped his arms around her. "I'm serious."

Did he really think she'd be interested after what happened to Lili? But Lili was alive and as cute as she ever was.

Janae reached for her phone. "Yes, Mr. Williams?"

He handed her phone back to her. "I'm glad you insisted the kids all go together." He rocked her in a slow rhythmic sway and hummed their song in her ear. "We could turn off the lights, and no one will know we're here."

"Or we could sit out here until the kids come home." She

turned away from him and hit the send button to post the pictures.

He nuzzled his lips against the back of her neck. "Or we could put the candy out for the trick-or-treaters, so they don't interrupt us."

Janae continued scrolling through her app. "Or we could answer the door for each and every one of them."

Ethan laughed before kissing her. "You are one stubborn woman. Maybe that's one of the things I love the most about you." He snatched her phone out of her hands.

"Hey, I wasn't done." She tried to reach for it, but he kept it over his head.

Tucking it in his back pocket, he said, "Come get it."

Janae wrapped her arms around his middle, the warmth of his body pressed into her and she melted against him. How could she stay mad at him for something that hadn't even happened? Yet, it was like waking up from a dream where he'd cheated on her, and she was still angry with him all day because of something he really hadn't done. Was this like that?

What if he betrayed her again and let Lili drown and then things would just go back the way they would be in the future? Could she take that risk?

She lowered her arms around his waist. "Can I please have my phone back?"

Ryan stumbled up the sidewalk, completely out of breath. "Mom! Dad!" He bent doubled over, breathing hard.

Ethan released Janae and put his hand on Ryan's shoulder. "What's the matter, bud?"

"It's Taylor. She got hit by a car!"

Janae's stomach dropped to her feet and her head buzzed. No, it was Grace who'd broken her arm, not Taylor.

"What do you mean?" Ethan asked.

Ryan was crying. "Oh, Dad…it's so bad. There's blood coming out of her mouth."

"Where is she?" Ethan took his hand, and they raced down the sidewalk; Janae following close behind.

Not Taylor, she wasn't supposed to get hurt. It was Grace she'd been trying to save. "What happened?" Janae asked, fighting the anxiety rising tight against her throat.

"Lili ran into the street. Taylor pushed her away from the car, and it hit her."

They rounded the corner to where a group of people had gathered. One man knelt next to the form on the ground. Blood pooled around her head.

"Taylor!" Janae screamed and fell to the ground beside her. "No, baby, come on. Wake up. Please be okay."

Ethan knelt on the other side and felt for her pulse. Shaking his head, the tears flowed down his face.

Janae shook Taylor's shoulders, her head flopping like a doll. "Wake up! I'm not going to let you die. I can't lose two of my children."

Ethan stood. He walked around Taylor and pulled Janae from their daughter, wrapping his wife in his arms.

The distant wail of sirens grew louder as the firetruck approached.

Janae's heart raced. "Make them wake her up."

The firetruck stopped at the curb and the paramedics grew into a busyness of activity as they checked for vitals then performed CPR.

An ambulance arrived and the crew continued to work on her.

Gripping Ethan's sleeves, Janae's heart stopped, her hands grew clammy, and her head buzzed.

After a few minutes, one of the men came over to them. "I'm sorry, there's nothing more we can do."

"No! Do something." Janae wasn't going to let them tell her Taylor was gone.

"We've done everything we can do. The doctor in the emergency room has radioed for us to stop trying to revive her. I'm so sorry."

Janae turned away from him, buried her head in Ethan's chest and sobbed. Ethan was originally going to take Lili trick-or-treating. They should have gone with them. Instead of her husband thinking only of his selfish needs, Taylor would still be alive.

Eventually the coroner's van arrived. When they lifted her onto the gurney, Janae's knees buckled. Ethan held onto her, his strong arms supporting her.

They covered her precious little girl with a sheet and carted her off like she no longer mattered to anyone.

A paramedic, with compassion in his eyes, handed Ethan a sheet of paper. "The doctor will have to sign her death certificate. Here are a couple of mortuaries you can contact to have your daughter taken to. On this side is a list of grief counseling agencies and clergy who specialize in dealing with the loss of a child. Is there anyone you'd like for us to call?"

Ethan shook his head and took the paper.

Panicked, Janae searched around her. "Where's Lili? Grace?" She searched the crowd for her daughters and found them standing on the sidewalk, their arms around each other. Tears streamed down Grace's face.

Janae ran to them and held both of her girls as if she'd lose them as well.

"This is all my fault," Grace cried.

"Oh, no sweetheart. It isn't." Janae knew where the fault lay. If Ethan had taken Ryan and Lili…

Grace sobbed. "It *is* my fault. If I had kept a tighter hold on her hand, she wouldn't have run into the street, and Taylor wouldn't have pushed her out of the way."

Ethan wrapped his arm around Grace. "Sweetheart, it wasn't your fault."

Janae tightened her jaw. No, it wasn't any of their faults. She glanced to where the police were talking to the driver of the silver Corvette, the same young man who'd been told time and time again to slow down in a residential area. She hoped he'd rot in prison.

After Ethan had contacted family, and arrangements made, Janae crawled into bed, and long into the night, she cried herself to sleep in Ethan's arms.

11

Friday, December 13, 2019

Janae rolled over in bed and pushed the blankets up to her eyes, dabbing at the tears that hadn't stopped flowing since last night. Would she ever feel normal again? Had she traded Taylor's life for Lili's?

"Wake up, sunshine, or you're going to be late!"

Who was talking to her, and why did she sound so chipper after the tragedy of last night? Janae sat up. It took more than a moment to register where she was. The same dreary apartment she'd awakened to yesterday surrounded her. Who was doing this to her? What kind of sick maniac played that kind of cruel prank on her?

Yet, she remembered working at Charity Dollar, and not just of the day she'd awakened to, but a whole series of patchy memories...like someone had poked holes in her brain and many of her days had leaked out.

Someone couldn't have planted those kinds of images in her head.

Ana stood over her bed. "You're going to be late for work."

Janae flopped backward and pulled the covers over her head. Not only was she divorced, she had two deceased children, a dingy apartment, a car that marginally worked, and her great-grandmother was her guardian angel. Was this an alternate reality? What happened tomorrow when she woke up? What day would it be then?

Ana patted her foot. "Let's get a move on. You don't want to lose this job, too."

Peeking out from under the cover, Janae watched as her guardian angel pulled the same black slacks and blue shirt out of the closet.

Janae slid out of bed and retrieved her phone on the nightstand, then dialed Ethan. He had to explain what was going on.

"We're sorry, the number you dialed is no longer in service."

Her stomach tightened, and the phone in her hand burned into her palm. She scrolled down to see if she had Taylor's phone number. Her heart sank when it didn't come up. Grace was still in her contact list, as was Ryan.

This craziness had to stop, and Grace had to provide answers.

"Hey sugar," Janae said when Grace answered her phone.

"Oh, hi Mom." Grace sounded different than she had yesterday.

Pausing to collect her thoughts on how to ask about Taylor, Janae trembled. "How's Dad?"

"Fine…" came her hesitant answer.

"And Ryan, how's he doing in school?"

"Good, I guess…" Again, her voice came out hesitant.

"That's nice to hear." Janae swallow. "And your other sister?"

"What are you talking about?" Her voice rose in volume and pitch. "I don't have any other sisters."

Now Janae wished she hadn't called her at all. "Look, honey, I didn't mean to upset you."

A long huff came from the other end of the phone. "What is the matter with you?"

Janae let out a relieved sigh. "Well, because, I don't have Taylor's phone number... I was hoping maybe..."

"Of course, you wouldn't have her number." Grace yelled into the phone and then hung up.

Janae slumped onto the bed, the tears threatening to scorch the back of her eyeballs.

As Ana buttered the toast, she shook her head. "You could have asked me about the other girls."

Afraid to know, Janae's eyes rose to meet Ana's.

Compassion filled Ana's eyes. "Lili drowned, and she's buried beside Taylor, who was killed in a car accident."

A knife of emotions slit her insides open, and she bled great tears from her eyes. "Then it's true; I've lost two of my children?"

Ana set the toast on the plate and handed it to Janae. "Sometimes we think we're in control of our destiny, when really we're not."

Janae set the plate in her lap. "Why then am I here, and why did I get sent back only to lose another one of my daughters."

"We don't have time to discuss all that right now." Ana motioned to the toast in Janae's lap. "We'll talk about it tonight after you get home from work."

"My daughter died last night. Don't I get one day to mourn her death?"

Ana handed Janae a tissue and sat on the bed next to her. "That was over six years ago, and you mourned enough to last a lifetime."

Janae took the tissue and dabbed at the tears streaming down her face. "But to me it happened yesterday."

Ana nodded. "Sometimes the pain feels so fresh." She patted Janae's hand. "Cry when you feel like it; smile when you feel like it; and don't feel guilty about either one."

Janae tossed the toast in the trash, set the plate in the single sink, and crawled back into bed. "Today, I choose to cry." The blade had slid up to her heart and twisted until she wished the knife was real.

Ana sniffled. "I know how it feels."

Janae rolled to the wall and curled her knees close to her chest. "How could you?"

"I've lost loved ones as well."

Janae's phone chimed, and she ignored it for a moment. Then deciding Grace may have called her back, she rolled over and checked the ID.

Work.

Running her sleeve over her eyes, she answered the phone. "Hello."

"Why you don't come to work today?" Mr. Chang asked.

"My daughter died yesterday." Never mind that it had actually happened so long ago.

A gasp on the other end preceded Mr. Chang's words. "Why you not call me and let me know? I help you with funeral. My brother have hearse."

His attempts at comforting Janae sent the knife plunging deeper. "I'm not coming in today." Then under her breath, she added. "Or ever." She pressed the end button and dropped the phone back on the nightstand and sobbed…for Liliana, for Taylor, for her broken marriage…for her life.

12

Much later when Janae awoke, Ana had left. The shadows in the room told Janae it was probably mid-afternoon. She dragged herself to the shower and turned the water as hot as she could stand it.

In the other room, her phone rang; its ringtone said Gina.

Dripping, she flung a towel around herself and stepped out of the bathroom to answer it.

"Mr. Chang called and said you didn't go in to work today." Why did her mother-in-law have to be so meddlesome? And why had her boss felt the need to call Gina? So, she missed a day of work. Did her mother-in-law worry that Janae might ask her for more money? Ha! That would never happen. Funny how she remembered Gina handing her an envelope with several twenties tucked inside. "Until your alimony kicks in."

Janae hated accepting the money and hesitated before taking the envelop, but she'd needed the money to survive until she got a job. A quick flash of another memory came to her. Mr. Chang had hired her after Gina had sent him a recommendation. She wished her other memories of the last five years came back as easily.

"Are you ill?"

"No, I'm not sick. I just couldn't go in today." Janae pushed a stray lock of hair off her forehead. "Don't I get time to mourn the loss of my children?"

Gina let out a soft huff. "Honey, you have got to stop letting these bouts of depression rule your life. If a person…"

Here came the series of condescending suggestions for her. If only it had been her mother instead of Gina. And yet, her mother-in-law had helped her out a multitude of times, even when she was still married to her son.

Gina asked, "Are you going through another episode?"

While Taylor's and Liliana's deaths had happened over five...or was it six years ago, for Janae, they were still fresh, the wounds too raw. "I just couldn't go to work, okay."

"Why don't I come over?"

"No..., I'm okay." Ha, that was a laugh. Janae couldn't remember the last time she was okay.

"Have you eaten? Do you want to go out?"

Did she? "No, I'm just going to stay home and watch a movie or something." The last thing she wanted or needed was another scolding from Gina.

"I'll be over in an hour."

"Mrs. Williams—"

Her mother-in-law hung up before Janae could argue. It was just like her to not listen. Taking a quick glance around her apartment, she decided she didn't care that it was a mess. Maybe she did care...a little bit. She used to care, especially if she thought Gina might drop in, like she'd done so many times while Janae was married to Ethan.

Living in this dumpy studio, her desire to keep her room immaculate had waned, if not vanished altogether. Looking around at the mess, she decided she would wait on the sidewalk so her mother-in-law wouldn't see what her place had become.

Janae leaned toward the bathroom mirror, noting the dark circles under her eyes and the wrinkles at the corners. Why did she feel so old? Doing a quick bit of math, Janae figured she would be celebrating her forty-fourth birthday in another month.

She applied enough makeup to cover her tear-swollen eyes and put on a blouse she'd remembered being one of her favorites. Although a little worse for the wearing, it was still comfortable and brought out the green in her eyes.

Once she dressed, she sat on the edge of her bed and opened up her Instagram. Maybe she'd posted tidbits of her life there. As she scrolled through her memories, Janae hadn't recorded much about her life in the last few years. A snapshot in front of the weathered store front of the downtown market, a plate of French fries and a hamburger, one of her leaning against the hood of Grace's car, and a picture of her hand with a broken nail taken shortly after her...divorce. That was the last time she'd had a manicure. Scrolling back to before Lili's death, she had created all kinds of videos and creative photographs of her life, her home, her children. All of them without Taylor and then more recently, without Lili.

After scrolling for what seemed like forever, Janae closed out of her app, slung her ugly purse over her shoulder and shut off the lights. With her jacket tight around her body, she stood on the sidewalk and waited. Why had she even agreed to have dinner with her mother-in-law?

When Gina pulled up, Janae dropped her phone in her purse and hurried down the sidewalk. The lingering sorrow followed closely behind her and joined her in the front seat. How did she explain to her mother-in-law the pain still so raw in her heart?

Janae got into the warm car and adjusted the vent.

Gina turned up the heat. "Mr. Chang said your daughter died today. He must have misunderstood."

Janae closed the door. "Yeah, probably. I meant that it just felt like it is all."

Gina reached over and put her hand on top of Janae's where it rested in her lap. "I miss them so much."

The knife blade kept digging into her—bigger, colder, and sharper with each twist in her heart. She hoped she'd wake up from this horrible nightmare. "Can we not talk about it?"

Gina removed her hand and put the car in drive. "Where would you like to go?"

"I don't care." Now that she thought about it, she *was* hungry since she had thrown her toast in the trash. Then between crying and sleeping, she hadn't eaten anything all day.

Gina turned the car onto the street. "Let's do Mexican," she said and headed toward her favorite restaurant.

Janae wished they'd ride in silence. She was still trying to process Taylor's death. Instead, her mother-in-law kept up a running monologue about her father-in-law's antics, his attempts at trying to change out the disposal and how he ended up calling a plumber after he busted the water pipe.

Picturing Bruce under the sink was something Janae would love to have seen. He never was much of a handyman, but that didn't stop him from attempting projects. They always ended up calling in the professionals. Ethan could have fixed it.

For the first time in ages, Janae felt the tug of a smile on her lips.

Gina turned into the parking lot. "It's nice to see you smile. You were always such a pretty girl."

"I'm hardly a girl anymore. I'm almost forty-four."

"Age is how you feel."

"Then today I feel a hundred and forty-four." Janae didn't wait for Gina's reply and exited the car.

After they had seated and ordered, Janae leaned back and watched the people around her all leading ordinary lives. Their conversations light-hearted, their voices cheerful. Janae envied them. It was like she'd gone to bed, then like Rip Van Winkle she'd awakened trying to figure out where she belonged in time.

Any future without her daughters was the worst kind of hell to live in.

13

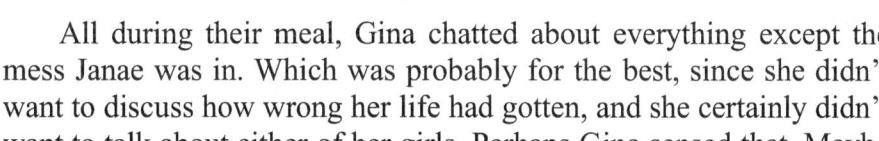

All during their meal, Gina chatted about everything except the mess Janae was in. Which was probably for the best, since she didn't want to discuss how wrong her life had gotten, and she certainly didn't want to talk about either of her girls. Perhaps Gina sensed that. Maybe it had been a good idea to take her mind off of her life. Although, thoughts of Taylor and Lili never left her mind.

Once Gina paid for their meal, Janae carried her leftovers in the Styrofoam container back to the car. For as hungry as she'd been, once she took the first few bites, her appetite left. Maybe tomorrow she'd warm up the leftovers...if there was a tomorrow.

The drive home was quieter.

Gina broke the silence in the car. "Any movie you'd like to see? We still have plenty of evening left."

Janae rubbed her brow trying to ease the headache building behind her eyes. "Not really. I think I'll just turn in early and catch up with Grace tomorrow."

Gina chewed her lower lip but didn't say anything. They'd always had an odd relationship. Janae never knew from moment to the next whether Ethan's mother liked her or if she was just being nice because of her son.

She wanted to ask Gina, but did Janae dare trust her ex mother-in-law with the weirdness she'd experienced the last two days? Maybe she would think Janae was crazy. It didn't matter what her mother-in-law thought; Janae had to know.

"What happened with Ethan?"

Gina took her eyes off the intersection and stared at Janae. "That's what I'd like to know. You've been so tight-lipped about it, that I've been afraid to ask, and Ethan isn't saying anything either."

Janae took a deep breath. "Please don't think I'm crazy or have me committed. But I woke up this morning somewhere in the future and I have no idea how my life got so shambled. How did I end up here?"

"You fell apart after Liliana's death." The light turned green, and Gina took her gaze from Janae and proceeded down the road. "Ethan tried—"

"No, Mrs. Williams, he didn't." Janae scratched her head at the hairline. "He grew so distant, and when we did talk, all we did was argue."

Gina shook her head. "The counseling you two went through, didn't that help at all?"

"Counseling?" She tried to remember a time when they'd sat down with someone outside of their marriage to get help. "What if I told you I've skipped almost five years of my life? They've vanished, and suddenly I wake up, and I'm here. My life is a mess; my kids won't talk to me; my husband..."

Gina let out a huff. "Why would you leave a good man like him?"

Janae rubbed her forehead with her fingertips. "I thought I could trust my husband."

The light turned red and Gina slammed on her breaks. "What are you talking about?"

"Two days ago, when you came to pick me up from work, I told you about him and—"

"Janae, we haven't spoken in weeks." Gina's hands gripped the steering wheel.

"You did. My car broke down and..." It was two days ago, wasn't it?

When the light turned green, Gina eased into the intersection. From the cross direction a truck barreled through the intersection slamming into the passenger side.

Betsy Love

14

Janae awoke to her stomach contracting like she was in labor. Moaning, she rolled over. That accident must have hit her hard in the abdomen for her to be feeling this way. Was she in the hospital? Did anyone care that she'd ended up there?

"Hey babe, are you all right?" Ethan sat on the edge of the bed and put his hand on her hip.

"You came?" Janae rolled to face her ex-husband.

"I heard you moaning." He put his hand on her abdomen. "Are you having more contractions?"

Janae put her hand over his, noting how swollen her belly was. "I'm pregnant?"

Ethan laughed. "You're just now figuring that out?"

Another contraction gripped her, and she moaned.

Ethan massaged the small of her back. "This is what we wanted, remember?"

Janae sat up, heaving her baby with her. "What day is it?"

"Tuesday."

"I mean, what year?"

"Sweetheart, seriously? It's not like you're Rip Van Winkle and have slept your whole pregnancy away." He stroked the hair behind her ear.

Another jump backward in time and she had no idea when. A fierce contraction hit her. "I think we better time these," she said breathlessly as the swell peaked. Which baby was she expecting?

Ethan examined his wristwatch. "Tell me when it's over and we'll time the next one."

She nodded and waited for the contraction to ease up. Once its grip lessoned, Janae took a look around the room. They were in Ethan's bedroom at his parent's house. So, this little one awaiting to be born was Grace, her first child. How had that birth gone? She remembered that everyone told her she would know when she was in labor. Even after reading every book she could about what would happen, she still had not been prepared for the pain. She couldn't lose Grace. Her oldest daughter was the glue that held her family together. What could Janae do to keep her daughter from dying? Isn't that why she'd been sent back to this time?

Another contraction started, blooming across her belly, and pulling from the bottom of her abdomen. "Time this." Again, the pain of it hit her.

They waited until the contraction ended. Ethan held his watch out for her to see. "That was only two minutes. Do you think we should go to the hospital?"

"No, let's time them for an hour and then call the doctor." If Janae remembered correctly, her water broke before they got to the top of the hour.

Sure enough, after fifty minutes, a gush whooshed out when she sat on the toilet. "Ethan?" she cried out from the bathroom, as the contractions intensified.

He popped his head in the door. "What is it?" Both excitement and fear were written on his face.

"Get my bag." Gasping for breath as another contraction hit, she said, "I think we should go to the hospital now."

Ethan ran from the room and hollered down the stairs to his mother. "It's time!" The excitement hung thick in his voice.

Janae stood and waddled into the bedroom. It was not fair at all to have to go through labor and delivery twice with the same child, but if it meant saving her girls, she'd go through this a hundred times if she had to.

Once they reached the hospital, Janae cried out as the baby

pushed against her cervix. An hour of transition and a few pushes later, Grace made her way screaming into the world. The doctor barely had time to put on his gloves to catch her. As planned, Ethan cut the cord and the doctor laid the most perfect, pink baby on her chest.

"Hey, little Grace." Ethan reached over and stroked her head, then leaned over and kissed the top of Janae's head. "Good job, Mama."

The doctor shook his head. "I can hardly believe this was your first baby. Most first-time moms usually take quite a few hours."

Three hours start to finish. Janae couldn't believe it herself, especially from all the reading she'd done. Yet, she remembered Grace's birth had gone quickly.

After making sure both Mom and Grace were stable, the hospital staff left the room to give the new family some quiet, private time.

Checking fingers and toes, and everything in between, Janae made sure her daughter was perfect. Ethan hovered next to the bed until Janae motioned for him to sit beside her.

He held Grace's knit cap in one hand and caressed the baby's head with the other. "She's beautiful, just like her mama."

Janae yawned. "I'm so sleepy."

"That was a lot of hard work." He lifted Grace from Janae's arms and moved to the chair beside her bed. "You go to sleep."

"Watch over her." Janae smiled, knowing why she'd been sent back to this time. This would be the perfect way to begin her duties as a parent, to protect her children and prevent both Lili and Taylor's deaths. Knowing what she knew now would give her that second chance all parents wished they had. Contented, she drifted off to sleep.

15

Friday, December 13, 2019

"Wake up, sunshine, or you're going to be late!"

No! She couldn't be back in her dingy apartment.

Janae jumped from her bed without even looking at Ana and grabbed her phone. Scrolling through the contacts, she found Grace's number. A moment of relief washed over her. Grace was fine. But why then was she here? Continuing through her contacts, she could find Ryan's number but not Taylor's. Hadn't she changed anything?

The woman patted her shoulder. "You have to get to work in thirty minutes."

"I don't have a job."

"Oh, but you do, and if you don't hurry, you'll be late." The woman pulled the same pair of black slacks out of the same tiny closet and draped them on the foot of the bed.

"How can I have come back to this time?" Janae rubbed her eyes and tried to focus on the shabby apartment. "I fixed things in the past, didn't I? I mean wasn't Grace where it all started?"

Ana chuckled. "Oh, heaven's no. It started much earlier."

"When?" Janae's heart pounded. "Can I go back there? Will that fix everything?"

The humor had left Ana's voice. "You can't just jump around time willy-nilly. You're here. Make the most of today and then see what to-morrow will bring." With that, Ana disappeared.

"Wait!" Janae shouted, but no one heard.

The neighbor upstairs pounded on the ceiling as if she might fall through any minute. Ana hadn't even fixed her toast like she had the other two mornings. Janae needed answers only Ana could provide.

Since Ana wouldn't answer them maybe Grace could fill in the details. Janae went back to her contacts and dialed Grace's number. "Hi sweetheart. Are you busy today?"

"Mom?"

"Yeah, it's me. I was just thinking about you and wondered if you'd like to have dinner tonight?"

"I have rehearsal at six." Hesitation filled her voice. "How about tomorrow?"

Disappointment filled Janae. "Sure." Tomorrow would never come.

"Where do you want to go?" Grace asked.

"You decide."

"The Broken Yoke," Grace said with no hesitation.

"Tomorrow at nine, then." Janae ended the call and set the phone on the nightstand. That had gone much better than the last time she'd spoken with her daughter.

The continued thumping in the apartment above let Janae know her neighbor was alive and kicking, literally. The sooner Janae left the building, the less she'd have to listen to whoever pounded on the floor.

She dressed, threw her hair in a ponytail, and headed off to work in the old clunker Honda that had once been Grace's. Did her father buy her a new car? He tended to spoil her. Or had Gina passed down another one?

Janae turned to view the dumpy apartment building. From behind the window over her studio, she caught the shadowy form of a woman bouncing around like she was dancing to some wild tune.

Tomorrow she'd set the alarm to go off earlier. If she got a tomorrow.

Like the last time she'd driven Grace's Honda, it wouldn't start until she'd pumped the gas several times. She missed her keyless start Mercedes.

Once more, Janae entered Charity Dollar. Mr. Chang stood with a duster in one hand and a box of candy in the other. After a couple of swipes, he replaced the open box. "You come on time today."

"I'm here." Janae went to the back office and donned the blue apron with the company name embroidered across the front. The bells on the front door jangled.

The customers entered the store. The exact same ones who'd came in day after day.

At her lunch break, her stomach rumbled. Did she have enough for lunch? She checked her bank account—barely enough to cover a couple of meals. When had her pay stub said she'd gotten paid? She pulled it out of her purse...every two weeks, and the date on this one said three days ago. She had to go another eleven days without money? How would she survive until then? Ethan had always provided enough for them to live quite well. Did she even have enough food at home to last that long? She'd have to make her money last.

Janae used her debit card and bought a nut-filled candy bar. That would have to hold her until she got home so she could go through her cupboards and assess her situation.

By the time Mr. Chang's wife arrived, Janae had been on her feet all day.

"You sell plenty?" Exactly as she did every night, Mrs. Chang came around the back side of the cash register and opened the drawer, checking the number of bills, then she ran a system scan of the register, verifying the total sales for the day. "Velly good. Too bad you not stay after Christmas."

"Thanks."

By the time she'd swept the floors and restocked the shelves, Janae just wanted to fall into bed.

"You come early tomorrow." Mr. Chang waved her out the door.

The bitter cold swirled around her. Janae wrapped her coat tighter, pulled the scarf across her mouth, and ran to her car. The starter grinded as she turned the key in the ignition. Why wouldn't it start? She pumped the gas a couple of times. Nothing she tried seemed to help. Was she hoping too much for her car to start, just one more time?

Several flakes of snow hit her windshield and stuck. She couldn't stay here out in the cold.

Janae bit her lower lip, then dialed. "Gina?"

"How nice of you to call."

"I have a problem."

"Of course, you do." Janae could practically see Gina roll her eyes.

"My car won't start."

"Did you try pumping the gas pedal…"

"Yes, Gina. Grace is at rehearsal." She started to say that Taylor was in Pine Bluff, then remembered that her grave lay next to Liliana's.

Before Janae could answer, Gina asked, "Are you at work?"

Janae shivered. "I just got off."

"Give me twenty minutes. I'm already in my pajamas."

By the time her mother-in-law arrived, Janae's teeth chattered and the feeling had disappeared from her fingers. She jumped out of her car and into the front seat of Gina's warm vehicle, then turned the air vents so they blew onto her face. "I'm sorry to drag you out at this time of the night. I really appreciate it."

Gina didn't say anything as she swung out of the parking lot and headed east.

They sat in silence. Janae just couldn't bring herself to have the same conversation about how wonderful Ethan was, and how Janae should have never let him get away.

When the light turned green, Gina eased into the intersection. From the cross direction a truck barreled through the intersection slamming into the passenger side.

16

Wednesday, July 10, 2003

The smell of bacon wafted through the house, teasing Janae's hunger. Ethan had a way of getting her out of bed on a Saturday morning. She could hear giggles from the other room. Janae sat up, hoping to find herself back in her bedroom in her beautiful home on Elm Street. A smile crept up her face. Perhaps, she'd finally awaken from her dream and she could get back to her usual life, except the giggles didn't sound like her older children. Grace's unmistakable laughter was from when she was much younger.

Moaning, the memory of last night hit her and she covered her eyes. The screeching of tires, the truck barreling into the side of Gina's car, then nothing.

Her nightmare hadn't ended. Where was she in her life this time?

A small child, maybe four, bounced onto the bed. "Mommy, mommy! I maked breakfast with Daddy."

"Careful, sugar." The mattress crunched when Ethan sat beside her. "Don't hurt the baby."

She thought they'd gotten rid of that bed when they moved into the house on Elm. She rolled over to face them; the weight on her stomach felt like someone had put a boulder in her belly.

Her protruding abdomen kicked at her hand where she placed it against her stomach. Pregnant? Janae struggled to sit up, twinges pulled at her. Ryan's labor and birth had taken forever. Did she want to go through this again? She pressed the heel of her hand against her forehead. When had she come to accept this odd reality of moving back and forth through time?

The little girl put her mouth on Janae's belly, her hands cupped around her mouth and hollered, "Hello, baby." Then to Janae she asked, "When?"

For a moment she studied the little girl's face—Grace. "Soon." The two-year-old in Ethan's arms must be Taylor. She reached out to take Taylor, wanting nothing more than to wrap her around her precious daughter, but the tightness of her abdomen made her roll back onto her side.

Rubbing her hands over her belly, Janae smiled at the little boy within. Ryan. They had deliberately not done a gender reveal so that they'd both be surprised when the baby was born. Ethan would be so excited when he got his boy after two girls. Not that he didn't adore his daughters, he wanted a little more testosterone in the family was all. "Even things out," he said.

"Are you hungry?" Ethan asked, and then rolled his eyes. "Dumb question. When aren't you?"

"Starving." Janae shifted to the edge of the bed and tickled Taylor's neck.

Suddenly, she felt a pop, and the bed soaked around her. So much for breakfast. If she remembered right, it wouldn't be until tomorrow morning that she got to eat. Would she be here long enough to meet her son for the second time? To see the look on Ethan's face at the blessing of a boy.

"It looks like Mommy is going to have the baby today." Ethan set Taylor on the floor and picked up Grace, setting her next to Taylor.

"Yay, baby, baby!" Grace danced from foot to foot.

Janae stood and waddled into the bathroom of their two-bedroom apartment. "You better call your mom." Those were the same words she'd said when she'd gone into labor with Ryan.

From the other room, Ethan spoke in excited tones to his mother. She could hardly wait to see the look on his face, tomorrow, late morning, after a grueling, long labor. It would be so worth it.

Once they arrived at the hospital, Janae went through the normal admissions process and slipped into the ever-so-lovely hospital gown. As the contractions gripped her belly, she wished that she could have gone back in time to the day after the birth. How could the universe curse her with being in labor for twenty-eight hours--twice?

The nurse pressed the stethoscope to her abdomen. "I'm not getting a heartbeat."

That's not how it had gone the first time. The baby's heartbeat had been strong. She had to change this now, or her baby would be stillborn, like the one between Ryan and Lili. "Maybe if you hook me up to the monitor."

With a neutral expression on her face, the nurse wrapped the belt around Janae, gooped up her abdomen, and then positioned the fetal monitor where the baby's heart should be. The nurse worked for several moments and still couldn't find a heartbeat.

"It's probably just this machine. I'll go get the technician."

Fear gripped her insides. This couldn't be happening. When she'd gone into labor with Ryan, things had been fine, though longer than she wanted. This was not at all how it happened.

When the technician arrived, Janae was having intense contractions.

The nurse pulled up her gown to reposition the monitor.

Ethan gasped. Blood pooled on the bed.

The nurse hurried from the room, while the technician adjusted the monitor and the settings on the machine. "I have a heartbeat," he finally said shaking his head. "But it's too low."

Within minutes the room became a buzz of activity. Both a doctor and an anesthesiologist came in. In hushed tones, Janae heard the words, cesarean section and fear struck her.

Janae reached out her hand to Ethan. "I have to tell you something. It's important."

"Sure, Babe, what is it."

"Protect our son."

"Son?"

Janae gripped his hand tighter. "Not just him, but Grace and Taylor and Lili."

"Lili? Who's that?"

73

As they whisked her away, Ethan's hand slipped from hers. A mask covered her face. She wanted to warn Ethan before it was too late.

Janae disappeared into the oblivion of anesthesia.

17

Janae opened her eyes and stared up at the blank ceiling. She didn't want to look around and see that she was once again forward in time. She wanted desperately to be in the hospital. Had they been able to save Ryan? Where was Ethan?

"Wake up sunshine."

Janae slammed her fist onto her mattress. "No! I don't want to be here."

As if Ana hadn't heard her, she went on. "You're going to be late for work." She pulled the same pair of black slacks and the plain blue shirt from the closet and laid them on the end of the bed.

Janae sat up. "Where's Ryan? Did the doctor save him?"

"Yes, he did just fine."

Relieved, she exhaled and put her hands on her face. At least she still had Ryan and Grace. Her heart ached for her other two children. "Why did you send me back to Ryan's birth and then have it turn out different?"

"Perhaps you needed to appreciate your son's remarkable birth."

A vise constricted around Janae's insides. "He almost died."

Janae picked up her phone, hoping that this time would be different because Ryan's birth was different, that Taylor's phone number would be in her contacts. Maybe her son's almost death had changed things. She scrolled through them, stopping when she ended at her work number. Could she take the day off, find her still living children and reconnect with them?

She hesitated for a moment before calling Mr. Chang. "I'm not feeling well."

"I dock your pay. You come Sunday. But be here at eight." Mr. Chang sounded irritated. Since it was the Christmas season, he'd needed help handling the extra customers. What would happen to her once the holidays were over? The Changs could go back to handling the store themselves.

Ana handed a plate with a slice of toast to Janae. "I suppose I could make you some scrambled eggs to go with that since you're not going in to work today."

Janae set the toast on the counter. "What is going on? Why would I be sent back to an alternate birth experience with Ryan and have him survive? Shouldn't he be dead like my other two children? What else are you going to torture me with?"

Ana pulled out a skillet from under the sink and set it on the two-burner hot plate. "What do you mean?"

Janae took the skillet from Ana and turned off the element. "With my life. One day I'm here, repeating the same stupid day, the next I'm suffering the tragedy of someone I love."

Ana didn't say anything, and Janae wondered if she'd heard her.

Janae stripped off her sweats and t-shirts and located her favorite jeans and blouse. "I'm going to spend the day connecting with my children."

"That would be wonderful. Good luck," Ana said and disappeared.

Janae wished she could go back to her prank theory, but with everything that had happened in the last several days—or was it years—she'd come to accept that her life was just plain weird. Maybe *accept* wasn't quite the right word. Maybe she was insane after all.

After spending enough time in the shower that the water ran cold, Janae dressed, then checked her contacts on her phone, breathing a sigh of relief when she reached Ryan's name.

"Hey bud, it's Mom."

"Oh, hi, Mom." He actually sounded happy to hear her voice.

"Are you on Christmas break yet?"

"Not for two more weeks."

She didn't want to wait that long; she'd probably end up back in time somewhere and never get the chance to tell Ryan how much she loved him. He'd been twelve the last time she saw him. "Can I stop by the school and kidnap you for lunch?"

The hesitation on the other line was palpable. "I've got this girl I'm meeting."

"Your girlfriend?" Janae had mixed emotions about him getting all tangled in a relationship at such a young age.

"Not yet, but I'm hoping."

"Maybe she'd like to come along." Janae tried to sound excited when all she wanted to do was spend time with her son without anyone else around.

"Can we meet tomorrow? I won't have basketball practice until after the Christmas break."

Disappointed, Janae tried to smile. "Sure, that sounds like fun." It would never happen since she was caught in a freaky time warp. The next time she went back in time, she'd tell him then. Would he remember it by the time he turned seventeen? She hoped he would.

"Pick me up after Dad leaves for work."

"He's still working weekends, huh?" Janae asked.

"You know Dad."

"Will Claire be at the office?"

Another long pause followed. "I don't know. Why would you ask me such a thing?"

Janae took a deep breath and exhaled slowly. "Forget it." She probably shouldn't ask the kids about their father's girlfriend. The thought made her insides quiver. "I'll see you around eight. Mimi's or Broken Yoke?"

"I don't care. You pick." Ryan's indifference came through loud and clear. What had Janae done that had all but alienated her children from her? Had Ethan poisoned their minds?

"Okay, sounds good." She paused for a moment. "Ryan..."

"Yeah?"

Then feeling embarrassed over telling him how much she loved him, she said, "Never mind. I'll tell you tomorrow." Janae ended the call. Taylor's phone number still didn't show up. Her stomach knotted as she scrolled back up to find Grace. With another sigh of relief, she dialed her oldest daughter.

"Oh, hi, Mom."

"Do you have class today?"

"Yeah. Next week is finals. I'm headed to Natalie's in a bit to study and then I have a class afterwards."

Janae nodded even though her daughter wouldn't see it. "She's sure been a good friend to you, hasn't she?"

Grace huffed. "Better than some people."

Janae suspected that comment was directed at her, but she pretended it wasn't. "Do you think you could break away and have dinner with me?"

"I have rehearsal for the Christmas show starting at six."

Why didn't Janae remember? "How about breakfast then. I'll pick you up at nine."

"Why are you acting like you care all of a sudden?"

The comment stabbed Janae to the core. Hadn't she been there for her children? Hadn't she been the one who mended her kids' aches and pains? "I do care. I have always cared." Please let her say yes. "Natalie can come if you think it would be less awkward."

"Sheesh, Mom. It will be more awkward with her there."

Janae pictured Grace rolling her eyes and pulling at the side of her mouth with her teeth. "Then I'll pick you up in a few minutes. Are you at Natalie's now?"

"No, I was going to head over there in a minute. So, pick me up from her house."

Janae breathed a sigh of relief. At least her daughter had agreed. Janae tried to remember what had happened that created such tension with her children.

Maybe if she could go back to her house, and wander around, she'd get some memories back. For whatever reason, she had to get to the n didn't want her around their father. She had to get to the bottom of what had happened.

18

Before rounding the corner to Natalie's house, Janae drove past the home Ethan had designed and built just for her. So much had changed. The trees stood much taller, the exterior had been painted a shade of gray-blue that Janae would have never chosen, and shutters had been added to the upper windows. Now even more, Janae wanted to take a look inside. Had Claire insisted on a change to the house? Maybe once they finished their meal, Grace would agree to let her go inside.

Grace stood out on the sidewalk, bundled in a fashionable jacket and leggings tucked inside a pair of snow boots. She'd colored her hair—dark brown with golden highlights looked stunning on her. When had her little girl grown into such a beautiful woman? Janae hoped Ethan was keeping a close eye on the guys dating her.

Her daughter opened the door, slid in and slammed the door closed twice before it latched. "Wow, Mom...way to take care of my car."

Janae chuckled. "Yeah, she's suffered a lot of abuse, hasn't she?"

"Hey, I only had that one accident, and Dad managed to get her fixed up pretty good."

"You were in an accident?" Janae reached out and gripped Grace's hand. "Are you okay?"

Grace pulled her arm back and rubbed her wrist. "I'm fine. It only hurts when it's cold."

"But you broke your arm on Halloween night...the night..." She couldn't bring up Taylor's death like this.

Grace narrowed her eyes. "No, I broke my arm in the accident last year."

Last year?

"Okay, I would have remembered your accident, wouldn't I?" Suddenly it dawned on Janae. "I was in the accident with you, and I must have bumped my head." Maybe that's why everything seemed so messed up and why she couldn't remember things.

"What are you talking about?"

"I don't know..." If she wasn't in the accident with Grace, why was she having such a hard time figuring out where in her life she was? "Did I ever hit my head hard enough to suffer from memory loss?"

"How would I know?" Grace turned the vents so they directed the air to blow on her face. "I hate this time of year. It's always so freaking cold."

Janae couldn't believe her daughter had changed so much in the last five years. "You used to love Christmas."

"You must have hit your head pretty hard." Grace let out a huff.

"I wish I could remember that, too." So, she must have had some kind of traumatic brain injury. That would explain the gaps in her memory. But going back in time...how could she explain that?

Janae's phone chimed and she checked the caller ID. Work. She silenced it and then shut it off. It no longer mattered that she had a job or that she'd get another chance to go into work on this strange time loop. Right now, it seemed that the only consequences she faced was the ones that mattered the most, and she couldn't even remember the choices she'd made that led up to her current situation.

Janae put the car in drive and headed toward the little café close by. She'd often kidnapped her children, excused them from classes, and treated them to a midmorning brunch. Mommy-daughter or mommy-son dates is what she called them. Ryan seemed to like them the best since it got him out of class. Grace loved them because of the food. It didn't matter to her which class she missed. Catching up for her was always easy.

Once the waitress seated them, Grace perused the menu,

drawing her eyebrows together. "Are you sure you can afford this?"

"Get whatever you want. I'll just work an extra shift at Charity Dollar."

Grace's menu hit the table when she released it. "You don't work at LaBaron Law office anymore?"

Janae didn't know what to say. "I, uh..."

"Don't tell me you got fired from that one, too."

Flopping forward, Janae rested her head on her folded forearms. "I can't remember anything."

"Dad said you'd gone crazy after Lili died." Grace took a deep breath and slowly let it out. "But I didn't know it had gotten this bad.?

Maybe there was truth in Grace's words. Maybe she had gone insane and she was just now realizing it. "What about the bump on my head?" As she glanced up at her daughter, moisture burned Janae's eyes. "Sweetheart, I don't know what's happening to me. It's like one minute I'm here, and the next I'm living in the past, a different one than what I remember."

Compassion filled Grace's eyes as she reached across the table. "Dad said there was nothing we could do, and we should just let you go."

"What? Why would he say that? I thought your father loved me. He vowed to love me through sickness and health. Why would he just throw me away? Wouldn't he stay with me even if I'd gone crazy because of an accident?"

"Mom, he didn't abandon you; you left us. You walked out on us."

Janae gasped. "I would never do that. Sure, your father and I had our disagreements, but I would never leave him."

Grace folded her arms over her menu. "I'll never forget the day you packed your bags and moved out."

"No... I didn't." Janae couldn't help the desperation in her voice.

"I. Was. There." Each word came out clipped.

Janae may have lost her love for her husband, but she would have suffered through her marriage for the sake of the kids. "Are you sure you're remembering it right?"

"I came home from school, and you were screaming at Dad. You told him you never wanted to see him again. You yelled at him and told him if Taylor hadn't died, Lili would still be here."

Rubbing her forehead, Janae tried to piece the events together. Nothing made sense. Was she insane? Did she have a mental breakdown? "Grace, honey, I would never have done that to you unless I was completely out of my mind."

The waitress came to the table. "Are you ready to order?"

Grace handed the menu back to her and rose from the table. "I'm not hungry anymore."

Janae stood and put her hand on her daughter's arm. "Wait, please, Grace. Don't leave me." She needed answers, and Grace was the only one who could tell her what happened before...

Graced pulled from Janae's grip. "Why? You left us, and now all of a sudden your life is in shambles, and you want me to figure it out for you?" She walked toward the door, her cell phone to her ear. "Natalie..."

The waitress's gaze went from Grace to Janae. "Can I get you anything?"

Janae shook her head and slumped back into her chair. "No, nothing."

19

After leaving the café, Janae drove the several blocks to her former employer. She parked in front of the law office she'd supposedly worked for. The building sported a rock front. The landscape, normally green in the summer, lay buried under a foot of snow. The parking lot had been plowed and the piles were shoved over the walkway. A *For Sale* sign hung between the pine trees in the middle of the property. So, she hadn't been fired, the company had probably gone under. Or maybe Grace and Ana were right. She *had* been fired or at least laid off, maybe because the company had moved to a bigger building. She pulled out her phone, ignoring the numerous calls she'd missed from Mr. Chang and one from her mother-in-law.

She located LaBaron Law in her directory.

"Law Group of LaBaron and Lerner," the receptionist said.

"Oh, so you've taken a partner?" That explained the move and name change.

"Yes, a few months ago. Can I help you?"

Did she dare explain who she was? Yet, she needed some answers. "Is Mr. LaBaron in? Can I see him?"

"I'm sorry, but he's out of the country until next week. Would you like to schedule an appointment with him?"

"No, I won't be around then... I needed to speak with him today."

"If you'll give me your name and phone number, perhaps he can give you a call if he checks in before he comes back."

"Never mind." Janae hung up the phone. She highly doubted the lawyer would take time out of his vacation to contact a former employee, especially if he'd fired her.

A traumatic brain injury, that's what it was. She had lost her memory and was just now snapping out of it. But what about the angel who'd come to her for the last four mornings in a row? Would she know what had happened to her? "Ana?" Janae called, expecting her great-grandmother to appear.

When she didn't, Janae put her head on the steering wheel. Who else would know what happened to her?

Mrs. Williams.

She dialed her mother-in-law's phone number.

"Where are you?" Relief exuded from her voice. "Mr. Chang said you never showed up."

Janae didn't even try to keep the emotion from her voice. "Gina, I'm scared."

"Are you all right?"

"No. Can I come over and talk to you?" She didn't try to hold back the tears choking her voice.

"Of course."

"I'll be there in a few minutes." Janae hung up and tried starting the car. Blast that pile of bolts! After stomping the gas several times, the car still wouldn't start. Resting her head on the back of the seat, she let the tears of frustration flow before calling Gina back.

Waiting for her mother-in-law to arrive, Janae hugged her coat tighter and shivered. She should have never turned off the car. Did she dare ask Ethan to help her make the necessary repairs to keep it running? Maybe her parents would consider it. They'd always been willing to help with whatever problem she and Ethan had faced when they were so dirt poor after they got married. She shook her head. Had any of her friends stuck with her? After opening up her Facebook, she went to her home page and scrolled through the feed. She couldn't find anything about an accident or insanity. Her life had been wiped out as if she didn't exist after the divorce. She'd have thought so except for the few recipes for simple meals for one, and cute decorating ideas on a budget.

The only pictures on her phone camera were old ones from before the divorce. The last one she'd taken was of her pristine nightstand. Janae straightened her hair, dug through her purse for some lip gloss, and then after making herself as cute as she could under the circumstances, she snapped a selfie. The caption under her post read:

My life as of today is nuts. How are you all doing?

Asking a question had always elicited interactions in the past. Now she'd find out who still followed her and who even cared any more.

Gina showed up fifteen minutes later. "What in the world are you doing here? I'd have thought this would have brought back too many painful memories.

Janae wished she had memories, then maybe her life would make more sense. She closed the door and leaned forward, her face in the warm vent. "I don't know...feeling confused, I guess.

"You're not having another breakdown, are you?"

With teeth chattering, Janae replied, "I don't think so." If only she could remember what had brought on the first one. "Did I get fired from LaBaron?"

Ethan's mom huffed. "You're lucky you didn't end up in jail."

"What did I do?" Janae couldn't imagine that she'd do something illegal.

"Falsifying records in a law office is never acceptable." Gina glared at her.

Janae chewed her lip. "It's bad, huh?"

Gina nodded. "Luckily, for you, it was Mr. LaBaron who caught it and not the client."

"Did I do it on purpose?"

"I don't think so." Gina reached over and patted her shoulder. "You've never done anything like that before."

That explained why Janae hadn't been able to find a better paying job than the dollar store. She squeezed her mother-in-law's hand where it lay on her shoulder. "Anyway, thanks for picking me up. What would I do without you? This is the fifth time you've bailed me out this week."

Gina cranked up the heater and directed the other vents toward Janae. "Fifth?"

"Oh, right, that's not what I meant." Janae momentarily forgot that she was reliving this day over and over again. It was all just part of her head injury.

Gina pulled out of the parking lot. "So why didn't you go to work?"

"I took Grace out for brunch." She didn't need to tell her that had gone abysmally.

"How are her rehearsals going? I bought an extra ticket in case you wanted to go."

"Why wouldn't I want to?" Janae figured their relationship had slipped, but she couldn't imagine not wanting to be part of her children's lives.

"Good. I'm glad. We have mid-section seats...it's a perfect view of the stage." Gina drove toward Janae's apartment. "I'll pick you up. It's in two weeks."

Janae wanted to ask what the production was and where Grace was performing but decided perhaps her mother-in-law would think her crazier than she was. And besides, she had more pressing questions.

Maybe if she asked her about her husband by beating around the bush, she might get some answers. "What happened with Ethan and me? I mean as you see it."

"What do you mean?"

How did she tell her mother-in-law the last thing she remembered was saying that she wished she was divorced? "I know that after Lili's death, things were so strained between us."

"That's hardly the word I'd use to describe it. You changed so much after Taylor died, and then Lili drowning like that, I suppose it was just too much for you to bear. Nobody blames you for breaking. My goodness, any of us would have."

"Ethan didn't."

"Don't blame him. He tried so hard to keep it together. He never let anyone see him cry. I guess if his family thought he had it all together, they wouldn't fall apart either." Gina drove down the familiar streets.

The roads hadn't been salted yet, and the ice lay thick in sections.

"Be careful. I don't want to be in another accident." Actually, she'd been in too many to count already that had either killed her or sent her back in time.

"What do you mean? You've never been in an accident." The light turned red and Gina slowed to a stop, the tires slipping. "I'm always careful." With her hands gripped on the steering wheel, she turned to Janae.

"I meant Grace." That sounded stupid. She wasn't even in the car with them. "I mean, like the one she was in... I'd hate to repeat that."

Gina shook her head. "Janae Marie, what is going on with you?"

"Everything. Absolutely everything about my life stinks. My kids hate me, the ones left living, my husband is dating his secretary. Look at where I'm living. I had a degree as a paralegal. Just because I chose to stay at home to raise my kids, shouldn't mean I'm too old for gainful employment."

"Ethan's dating Claire? That's interesting."

Had her mother-in-law heard anything she'd just said? "Interesting? Gina, seriously. How long do you think he's been having an affair with her?"

"Ethan would never do that to you. You're the one who left him. He's a good man—"

"When he's cheating on me?"

Gina took her foot off the pedal and eased into the intersection. "You're the one who—"

The crunch of metal on metal filled the car.

20

Friday, September 13, 2010

Not again. Janae lay still trying to figure out where she was. What period of her life had she awakened to this time? She didn't want to open her eyes.

"Janae?" Ethan called from the other room, his voice muffled.

Wherever she was, or should she say whenever she was, she was still married to her husband. Did she want to be? From the sound of his voice, she wasn't sure if this was a happier time or not. She dragged herself out of bed and looked around her room. The paint still smelled fresh on the walls. The floral arrangement wasn't on the dresser, the bedspread was the same as the one they'd had in their apartment. Moving boxes filled their room and the dresser lay empty.

This had been a perfect day. The movers had delivered everything the day before and all she had to do was spend the day unpacking and organizing. Most important, she still had all her children alive and well.

Alive!

Well!

Janae jumped out of bed and tried to run down the stairs to see if the kids were in the family room watching TV. Nausea hit her before she reached the landing. She turned around and raced back upstairs straight to the bathroom where she knelt over the toilet. Morning sickness.

With her hand over her belly she traced the slight bulge. "Hello my little Liliana. I can hardly wait to meet you." Her rainbow baby had brought back so much joy after the stillbirth of their son.

"How do you know it's a girl?" Ethan held her hair away from her face.

False alarm. Probably from getting up too fast. "I don't know, just a sense, I guess."

"It could be a boy, then we could even out the team. Two little yous and two little mes."

"Or we could just outnumber you." Janae stood up.

His arms wrapped around her. "I'm still hanging on for another boy."

"Keep dreaming." She tried to remember the events of this day. The kids had gone swimming while she and Ethan sat at the pool's edge talking about...what had they discussed? "Are you going to the office?"

"No, I'm going to stay here and get my den set up." He kissed her on the forehead and left the bathroom.

Janae followed behind him. "I hope you'll help me arrange the living room. I'm not sure I like it the way it is. I'd like to get some photos put on Instagram this afternoon."

"We can get to it quicker if you help me in here," he said from the doorway of the den.

"In a minute. I want to check on the kids."

Grace, Taylor, and Ryan all sat on the couch, each with a bowl of cereal in their laps. They could have cleared off the table so they wouldn't be eating on her brand-new couch. Three pairs of eyes sat glued to the television. Janae studied her children's faces. Her oldest would be almost twelve, Taylor ten, and Ryan would turn seven in a couple of weeks. She would be planning a huge pool party with all the new friends he'd make in the neighborhood. Ryan always got along with people and loved meeting new friends.

"Hey, you three," Janae said.

"Hi, Mom." Ryan was the first to tear his gaze away from the screen, the look of trouble on his face. "Dad said we could eat in here, cuz there's no room on the table."

Janae punched her hands on her hips. "Would it have been so hard to move a couple of boxes?" She took the bottom of his shirt and wiped the milk running down his chin. "I won't be happy if you make a mess on my leather couch." She should be ecstatic that all of her children were alive and well, but the thought of them making her home a disaster before they even got settled irritated her.

Grace looked up for a moment. "Daddy says if it gets hot enough today, we can go swimming."

Janae shook her head. "I don't think so. We have too much to do before we can play."

"Awww," three little voices groaned.

Maybe she was being too hard on them. "I'll tell you what. Let's get the kitchen table cleaned off, so we can actually eat in here. Then maybe tomorrow we can take a break and go swimming." She had all three of their attention now.

"Yay!" they squealed in delight.

In the process of their glee, Ryan dumped his bowl, milk seeping down through the crack between the cushions.

A look of dread crossed his face. "Oh, no, Mommy. I'm sorry."

"Ryan! Could you be any clumsier?" She stripped off his shirt and wiped up most of the milk. "Grace, go grab the paper towels." Then to Ryan she said. "This is why we eat at the kitchen table."

Tears welled up in his eyes. "But there's no room on the table."

Janae scrubbed the tears rolling down his face with the milky shirt. "You put that bowl in the sink. Your breakfast is done."

"But I'm hungry."

Janae pointed to the kitchen sink. "Go, now." She turned to her daughters. "You two get the boxes off the table. I don't want to catch you with food anywhere in this house but at the table. Do you understand?"

Grace and Taylor stood and carried their bowls to the counter, then went to the kitchen and struggled to set the heavy boxes on the floor.

They were old enough to know the rules. "Wash your dishes when you're done. I'm going to go check on Daddy." Just because they were in a new house did not give them the right to think things would be different. If anything, Janae was going to be harder on them to keep their home from looking like they didn't care.

She left her children to clean up, then headed up the stairs. She popped her head into Ethan's den. Stacked boxes surrounded him where he lay under the desk running cords to his computer.

Janae bent down. "Ryan spilled milk all over the couch, and I've got to find the box with the Murphy's oil."

"I'm sure it was an accident."

"Don't defend him." Here he went again with always taking Ryan's side. Just because he was Ethan's only son didn't mean that he could get away with his poor choices and behavior.

Janae knelt next to his legs. "I can help you for a minute, and then I really need to make sure that the mess got cleaned up properly."

Ethan propped up on one elbow. "Do you know which box my keyboard got packed in?"

"Didn't you label it? I'm pretty sure I didn't." Then, as if seeing Ethan for the first time in forever, she examined his tight-fitting jeans, his bare chest, and disheveled hair.

"Can you look? I don't want to stay under here all morning."

"I don't know, you look kind of sexy down there."

Ethan took her hand and pulled her beside him. Turning to face her, he whacked his head on the bottom side of the drawer.

"See, I told you, it's a little cramped." She snuggled in closer to him, her lips close to his.

He closed the distance and caressed her lips with his.

Butterflies whirred in her stomach, and she responded to his kisses like a hungry teenager. How could she be angry with him when at this moment all was well in paradise? Except for the milk in the cushions. She should go look for that cleaner.

Janae pulled away, gazing into his eyes. The shadows from the desk above hid his face in the half light. Even in the darkness, the hunger in his eyes was unmistakable.

"Want to sneak away to the bedroom while the kids are watching television?" He toyed with her lips again, teasing her into submission.

Why could she never think clearly when he held her like this? All she wanted to do was give into their passion. Again, she pulled away from him, hating to break the spontaneity. "I have to tell you something."

He ran his hand down her neck, stopping at her collar bone.

"That you're crazy about me, and can't wait to make wild passionate love to me?"

"Besides that." Janae locked her fingers around his to stop them from exploring. "I need you to listen to me, because this is a matter of life and death."

Ethan drew his eyebrows together. "Why all of a sudden are you so serious? You're such a mood killer."

"I will make wanton love to you." She kissed his lower lip. "Just listen for a minute, alright?"

He brought her hand up to his lips and kissed her fingertips. "This is important for you to tell me right now?"

Janae nodded, thinking about her baby nestled in her abdomen. "The baby I'm carrying is a girl. Her name is Liliana. When she's five years old she will drown in our pool." She swallowed, dreading what she had to tell him. "You're supposed to be watching her, but you get distracted." Janae swallowed the hurt. "Lili slips under the water and drowns."

Ethan released Janae and drew back from her. "That's some crazy dream you had."

"It wasn't a dream." She didn't know if she should tell him about her time traveling. He'd think she was crazy. "Ethan, don't ask me how I know this, I just do, okay?"

"Your dreams are always more vivid when you're pregnant." He stroked the hair away from her face. "You know I will do anything to protect our kids."

"I know, just promise me." Her stomach tightened, and her heart raced.

"I promise."

Maybe if in the future, Ethan paid closer attention to Lili, they could save her and maybe fix this whole horrible mess they were in.

When Janae didn't answer, he brought his hand to her face. "I promise I'll do whatever I can to protect our children." His hand drifted down to her abdomen. "You think it's a girl?"

"I know it is."

"So, Ryan and I are going to be outnumbered once more." He kissed her again, this time longer, the hunger lighting a fire in her as well. Ethan had listened to her, taken her seriously. She closed her eyes, letting the warmth of his caress surround her.

The sound of shattering glass and a scream from downstairs broke their moment.

Janae sat up fast, smacking her head just like Ethan had, except she saw stars for a moment before everything went black.

21

Friday, December 13, 2019

Janae snapped the covers off her, gasping for breath. "No!" she yelled into her empty bedroom. Who? Who had screamed after the shattering of glass? Was that Grace's voice? It couldn't have been a cup or a plate, this had sounded louder, like maybe the sliding glass door.

"Ana?" Janae hollered. Her angel was nowhere in sight. Shouldn't she already be here picking out her clothes for work, just like she had on the other mornings? Why abandon her now?

She unplugged her phone and scrolled through her contacts. Grace was still there...Ryan--where was he? Why didn't he show up? Sixteen-year-olds had phones. Taylor was still missing as well.

She dialed Grace's number. "Hi, Mom. You're calling pretty early."

Janae's heart pounded. Please let him be alright; let this be a fluky thing. Maybe Ethan had decided not to pay for another phone; maybe for some silly reason Janae simply didn't have Ryan in her contacts. The words stuck in her throat, but she had to get them out. She had to know. "Where's Ryan?"

The time between her question and Grace's answer dragged on. Why wouldn't she just tell her?

"You've got to be kidding me," Grace finally answered.

"I have to know. Did he die?"

Grace exhaled sharply. "Did you take your medication?"

"How?"

Again, the silence on the other end of the line stretched for eons. "I don't have time for this. I have a huge paper due this afternoon."

"Wait, Grace, don't hang up. What happened?"

"Call Dad." She hung up.

"I don't have his phone number," she said to the beep signaling the end of the call.

"Ana, where are you?" she hollered again.

Ana appeared at the foot of the bed. "Oh, you're up early. You'll have time for a shower after all."

"I'm not going to work." She paced the small space.

"If you don't show up, this is another job you'll lose."

Janae stopped in front of Ana. "It's seasonal, I'm going to lose my job anyway." Pausing, she remembered that Ana had told her about Lili and Taylor's deaths. "What happened to Ryan?"

Ana took Janae's hand and led her to sit on the bed, then she sat beside her. "The girls were angry with Ryan for spilling the milk and Grace shoved him into the sliding glass door. She hadn't meant to hit him so hard. The door shattered. A shard hit his carotid artery. He bled out before the paramedics arrived."

"No, no, no! How can one family lose so many members? How can I go on with my life?"

"You still have Grace."

Janae pressed her hands into her forehead as if trying to remove the memory. "And she's not talking to me. She hung up on me; she leaves me sitting alone in the restaurant. What kind of mother-daughter relationship is that?"

"The kind that needs mending." Ana continued to hold her hand. The warmth should have been soothing under any other circumstances. How many people had visits from an angel and their life got worse, not better? Only Janae's.

"Why am I losing my children only to end up back here, where I get into an accident that sends me back in time? And every single time, it's horrible."

Oh, wait! Suddenly everything came clear. Ana wasn't an angel at all. She was the devil dressed up all cute and fancy like her grandmother.

Anger ripped her insides, like she'd swallowed razor blades. Janae jerked her hand out of Ana's hold on her. "Tell me the truth. Have I died and gone to my own personal hell, and my punishment is that I'll spend eternity losing my family members?"

22

Ana smiled at her for such a long time that Janae wondered if her demon was debating on whether to tell her the truth or not. "I'm not allowed to give you any information about why you're here. I'm only allowed to serve as an advisor."

Janae huffed. "Well, you're terrible at it! All you've done is set out my clothes, tell me I'm going to lose my job, and tell me which of my children had died. I hardly think that much is in the category of advice. If I could understand why I'm here, then maybe I could fix whatever it is I've screwed up and just go back to the right time in my life."

Moving to the closet, Ana chuckled. "Is there ever a right time in our life?" She pulled out the black slacks and ugly, blue shirt and laid them on the end of the bed.

Janae shoved the clothes onto the floor. "I told you, I'm not going into work."

"Suit yourself." Ana shrugged then vanished.

Her phone chimed. Grace. "Mom…I, um…I'm sorry I hung up on you like that. Do you want to meet on your lunch break? I can turn in my paper early and then skip class this afternoon."

Tears filled Janae's eyes, but she fought to keep them out of her voice. "I'd love to."

"How about that Italian restaurant around the corner from your work?"

Janae swallowed. How could she tell her daughter she wasn't there?

"I'm working somewhere else."

"You're not at LaBaron Law office anymore?"

Janae didn't know what to say. "I, uh..."

"Don't tell me you got fired from that one, too."

"I, uh…yeah..." Janae wished she could remember what had happened with her last job and what nearly sent her to jail. It couldn't have been as awful as her mother-in-law made it sound.

"So where are you working?" Grace asked, the irritation pouring through the phone.

"Charity Dollar Store on Main and Central." Janae said it so quietly she wondered if Grace had heard her.

Grace blew out a huff. "Well, at least you're employed."

For now. Which was one step closer to homelessness, and that would happen after Christmas. Changing the subject, Janae said, "I'm going to take the tram today since my car is acting funny. We can eat at that Chinese restaurant close by."

"Shall I pick you up around one, then?" Grace asked.

"Yes." She wanted to keep Grace on the phone longer, just to hear her voice. The last time they'd had brunch together Grace had stormed out on her. Today, she'd keep the conversation light; ask her about her classes, the production she was in. She'd steer her conversation away from Grace's siblings—the ones who'd passed away. If what Ana had said about Grace being responsible for Ryan's death, she'd especially steer clear of that.

Janae scooped up her clothes and threw them back on the bed, then took a quick shower.

Once she stepped off the tram close to Charity Dollar, the brisk air pushed its way under her coat. Janae shivered and pulled the collar tighter around her neck. Racing across the pavement, she slipped on a patch of black ice and caught the fender of one of the parked cars. That was close. The last thing Janae needed was another bump on the head sending her back to Grace's death. She just couldn't lose Grace, too.

Her stomach lurched. Is that what will happen at the end of the day? The accident tonight will send her back in time only to be unable to save Grace? Janae sat on the ice where the moisture seeped through her pants. What if when she went back this last time, she did nothing to stop events, or try to alter them? Could she put a hiccup in her time continuum and stop this crazy loop?

"I'm here," Janae said as she entered the store.

Mr. Chang looked up from the boxes he was shelving. "You early today."

"I wanted to put in an extra hour so that if you don't mind, I can take a longer lunch break." She walked to the back office not waiting for Mr. Chang to tell her no.

After putting on her apron, she went to where her boss was stocking candy canes. "I can finish that for you."

The door chimed and Mr. Chang nodded to the customers. "You help them. I do this."

Janae went to the young mother with a child on one hip and the other with her hand clutched firmly in hers. "Can I help you find something?"

The woman's face had a drawn expression. Under her thin coat, the woman's frame looked as if she hadn't eaten well for a long time. The children, too, looked under-nourished. "I'm looking for something the kids can take to their father."

"Is he overseas?" Janae asked. That was a dumb question. How could they take it to him if he was out of the country?

"Um, no..." She hesitated. "He's..."

"In jail," the older one piped up.

Janae didn't know they allowed gifts to be taken into a prison.

The woman must have seen the surprise on Janae's face. "He's not in jail now. He was released last week and is in a halfway house until he's cleared by his probation officer to come home."

She wanted to ask what his crime was but didn't want to offend the woman. "Let's see what we can find."

As they walked down the men's aisle, the woman rejected each item Janae offered. She could tell the woman had little money as she handed the items back after checking the prices. They moved on to the clothing aisle. Again, nothing seemed to be within her budget.

Janae stopped at the end of the aisle.

The woman hesitated and looked down at the little boy holding her hand. "I saw a survival kit on Amazon, and I was hoping I could find something similar."

It would definitely be cheaper here. "I think I know what you're talking about." Janae led her to another aisle that had a few sporting goods. She held up a vinyl pouch, unzipped it and held it out to the woman.

She took it from Janae. "Yes, this is almost exactly like the one I saw." When she turned it over to look at the price, her face fell. "Maybe we'll just get him a package of Tootsie Rolls. They're his favorite candy."

Janae rang up the small package and the mother left with her purchase. The baby on her hip cried when the cold air hit her face.

23

Janae chewed her lip. How could she afford to take Grace to lunch and still get by on what was left in her bank account before she got paid again? Maybe it didn't matter anyway because if this time loop kept going the way it was, everything would reset. She'd still have the same amount of money, lunch with Grace would have never happened.

For a moment, she eyed the register. It didn't matter if there were no consequences, right?

When Mr. Chang went to the back of the store, his feather duster in hand, Janae opened the cash drawer and slipped a twenty into her pocket. A twinge of guilt washed over her for a moment. She looked up to see if her boss had seen what she'd done. He had his back to her, busily dusting a shelf. She wouldn't take it tomorrow, or rather when she repeated this day. Maybe she wouldn't even come into work. It wasn't like it mattered.

What would life be like if it were free of consequences? Could she get away with all kinds of things?

Her chest tightened, thinking about Liliana, Taylor, Ryan. If she'd done things differently, her children would still be alive. Did her choices change the consequences? Yes, and for the worse.

Janae leaned against the counter and tucked her hand in her pocket, holding onto the bill. Was this a test that would put her deeper in Hell? For today she wouldn't care about what happened with her choices. It wasn't like it mattered.

She glanced around the store, hoping to see Ana. Angel or demon, maybe she'd have some words of advice. Wasn't that what she was supposed to do?

She pulled her hand from her pocket, leaving the money still tucked inside. Only after Mrs. Chang counted the drawer later that night would she find the missing amount. Couldn't she just tell her she got swindled by one of her customers? It happened a lot in stores like this. Mr. Chang would probably fire her. But that wouldn't matter because tomorrow would never come. She could take twenty-dollar bills from the till all day and it wouldn't matter, would it?

Janae bit the inside of her mouth. Maybe she should put it back. She reached into her pocket again.

Her stomach growled since she'd decided not to purchase the candy bar like she'd done the day before. That would buy at least four packages of cheap ramen, or two boxes of mac and cheese. She shuddered at the idea she had been reduced to eating like she and Ethan had when they were newly married.

Mr. Chang stood beside her. When had he finished dusting? "You ready to go to lunch?"

She took her hand out of her pocket again, the money once more left there. "Almost."

Mr. Chang pointed to the window. "Is that your daughter?"

Nodding, Janae took off her apron, ran to the back of the store and grabbed her coat. Then hopping inside the late model Mercedes, she noted Grace had the seats warming and the heater blowing. "Nice car." Janae tried to ignore Mr. Chang standing at the register chatting with a customer. *Only for today.* Tomorrow...

Grace took her foot off the break and headed across the parking lot toward the street. "This used to be yours."

Oh, right, the car. Janae turned her attention to her daughter and tried to decide the best way to proceed and not make herself sound like she was crazy. "I'm glad you got my car."

"You didn't think so after the divorce."

"Maybe I've changed my mind. Driving your Honda brings back so many memories of when your grandmother first gave it to you." She wouldn't mention how irritated she'd been with Ethan for allowing his mother to dote on their daughter in the first place. It set precedence so that the other children would expect one on their sixteenth birthday. Janae didn't want to talk about their vehicles. "So, how are your classes going?"

Grace pulled out of the parking lot and onto the busy street. "Great, except for microbiology."

Janae wished she could remember what field of study Grace had chosen. "What about it makes it hard?"

Grace puffed out her cheeks and blew out a huff. "The terminology. There's so much to remember."

"I can imagine." Janae hoped her daughter would say something about her course of study. "You've chosen a hard field."

"Nursing's not that hard; it's just some of the classwork..."

"Nursing?" Janae almost shouted in relief, but contained her enthusiasm when Grace shot her a look that said, "my mother is nuts." "I mean, you'll be an amazing nurse. You've always had such love and compassion for people. And you're a really good student; you always have been."

"Thanks!" Grace sounded sincere.

Maybe connecting like this would give Janae the help she needed to figure out where her life had gone so wrong. First, she needed Grace to open up to her. Not like the last time they'd tried to have brunch. Janae cleared her throat. "So, how's your play going?"

Grace's shoulders dropped as if the weight of the world had landed on them. "I'm about ready to drop out."

"That's too bad. I really wanted to see you."

Grace's burst of laughter surprised Janae. "Since when have you shown interest in my extracurricular activities? Haven't you hounded me about focusing on my degree?"

Janae wanted to reach over and take her daughter's hand like she had when she was a little girl. Instead she kept them clasped in her lap. "Can't a mom have a change of heart? Besides Grandma bought a ticket for me."

Grace gave Janae a dubious look. "Okay, what is going on?"

"Nothing. I just wanted to have lunch with my daughter."

The lunch crowd had died down, and the hostess seated them in the back corner. Janae always loved this spot the best, like they were secluded from the world. Ethan had brought her here several times, and they had enjoyed the intimacy of the cozy setting.

The waitress appeared and set two menus in front of them. "What can I get you to drink?"

Normally, Janae would have ordered a hot chocolate with raspberry flavoring. Today, with her limited funds she said, "I'll just take water with lemon."

"I'd like a strawberry-mango lemonade."

"I'll get those right out to you." The waitress turned and left the table.

Janae opened her menu and searched for the least expensive dish.

When the waitress returned with their drinks, Janae ordered the vegetable noodle dish that came with egg rolls and egg drop soup. If she ordered the brown rice, even though she preferred the fried, it would sit heavier on her stomach and make her feel fuller for longer. She'd eat the soup and rolls extra slow, claiming to not be so hungry. Then she'd take a few bites of the noodles, and box up the rest for dinner. That way she could get two meals.

Grace on the other hand, threw budget out the window and ordered Mongolian Beef, with a side of crab puffs. Still the total would come to over the twenty dollars she'd taken from her boss. Maybe Grace would volunteer to leave a tip. If not, they were going to have one rather unhappy server.

The waitress took the menus and left the table.

Janae took a sip of her water, then set the glass down. What kind of questions could she ask Grace? She had changed so much since high school; she had maturity written all over her face. Did she dare ask if she had a boyfriend?

Before Janae could ask, Grace asked one of her own. "So, how's your new job going?"

"Good, I suppose."

Grace nodded. "I hope you can keep this one."

Janae shrugged. "That would be nice, except it's only seasonal."

"It's too bad about your job at LaBaron, huh? What

happened?" Grace asked.

Not wanting to talk about it, Janae took a longer sip of her water. "Let's just say I'm not there anymore."

"That's too bad. You really liked that job."

24

Grace plowed through her lunch like she'd never had to worry about where her next meal was coming from. Janae smiled wryly. She hoped her daughter never had to worry about things like that.

Janae ate slowly, like she'd planned, so she'd have enough to take home for dinner.

The waitress brought the bill. Nineteen dollars and fifty-eight cents. Janae slipped the money from her pocket and held it for a moment before setting it inside the payment folder. "You wouldn't happen to have a couple of dollars, would you?" she asked Grace.

"Gosh, I'm a little cash poor until Dad gives me my allowance." She arched her eyebrows. "Don't you have enough?"

"It's fine. I'll run it on my card." Janae removed the cash and replaced it with her credit card. She'd put the twenty back when she returned to the store.

They still had a few minutes before she had to get back to work.

Janae took another sip of her water and studied Grace. Where had Janae been the whole time her daughter was turning into a woman? Had Janae really lost her mind after the divorce, after Lili's death... or was she sane and trapped in some kind of alternate reality.

Maybe she was dead after all. She'd heard that time wasn't linear in the afterlife. If she was living in Hell, then her jaunts back and forth were her eternal punishment. If that was the case, then why did any of her choices matter? But what if she needed to learn valuable lessons?

Grace picked up her purse and flung it over her shoulder. "Ready?"

Janae huffed a short laugh. "Ready for what?" Ready for Grace's death? Ready to jump through time again? Ready to keep living in this hell of a nightmare?

Easing from her chair, Grace scowled down at Janae. "To go back to work."

Janae stood and retrieved her own purse. How could she change her relationship with Grace? Wasn't this part of the problem? Is this why Grace hadn't died...yet? Her fingers clutched tight around the strap of her purse, and she took a deep breath. "So, I went to dinner with Grandma the other night, and she said we were barely speaking."

With her mouth twitched to the side, Grace reminded Janae of the times when she was little and was pondering some deep thought. "It's been hard on all of us since you and Dad split."

Janae felt like she was suddenly in a faceoff with her daughter. "Has your father been filling your head, trying to ruin our relationship?"

"No!" Grace pulled her eyebrows together. "Why would you think that? You left us, remember?"

Janae didn't want to discuss the past where everyone around them could listen in, so she headed toward the door.

Once they got in Grace's car, Janae turned to her. "Can I tell you something and you won't think I'm crazy?"

Grace snorted. "Mom, you haven't been right in the head for the last five years."

"Then tell me what happened, because I feel like I just woke up this morning from a long sleep and somebody else has been living my life."

Tears filled Grace's eyes. "You have not been yourself since Lili died, but then again, none of us have. For you, it's just like what you said, someone else had taken over your mind, and we don't even know who you are any more."

"That bad?"

Grace nodded. "It was like something snapped and you haven't been the same since. That's when you left Dad."

How could she fix this mess? "I think I'm finally back to me." Except for the part where Janae had stolen the money from her employer. Under normal circumstances she would have never done anything like that. Determined, Janae felt her pocket. She'd return it the minute she had the chance.

Grace started the car and cranked up the heater. "That's good to hear, except that it's kind of too late."

"Yeah, I know." The knife in Janae's heart twisted deeper. "Then you know about Claire."

"Claire," Grace repeated.

Unsure of the tone in Grace's voice, Janae asked. "Do you like her?"

"I guess she's alright." Grace pulled out of the parking lot, heading back to the dollar store. "What has she got to do with Dad?"

"Someone told me they are seeing each other."

"That's news!" Grace shook her head.

25

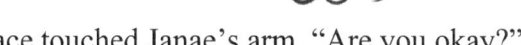

Grace touched Janae's arm. "Are you okay?"

"I haven't been okay since..." How long ago was it she lost Lili, then Ryan, and then Taylor? No, first it was Lili, then... "I am insane, aren't I?" Janae took Grace's silence as confirmation.

When they reached the store, Grace pulled into a spot close to the front and put her car in park. "I wish things were different. It just seems so unfair for one family to lose so much."

Janae had been thinking the same thing. "Next time you talk to your father, tell him I'm sorry."

Her oldest daughter's head hung. Janae wanted to wrap her arms around her like she'd done so many times when Grace was growing up. How much easier it had been to mend a scraped knee.

Janae stood for a long while staring at the tail of Grace's car as she left the parking lot. Grace was her last living child. Janae hadn't even gotten to say how much she loved her. Regret choked the breath from her lungs. She pulled her phone from her pocket and dialed Grace. It went straight to voicemail. "Grace, baby. I just wanted you to know how much I love you and how very, very proud of you I am. Never forget that. Ever. No matter how much I've messed up my life, I love you."

Janae hung up, ran to the bathroom at the back of the store and flopped down on the floor, letting the tears course down her cheeks. "Why?" She pulled her knees up to her chest and wrapped her arms around them, her head dropping on top of her wrists.

Ana touched the back of her head. "Sometimes when we get what we want, it's not what we really want after all."

"I didn't want this." Janae sniffled through her tears.

"Well, actually, if I remember right, you said, and I quote, 'I wish I was divorced.'"

As Janae released her hold on her knees, her legs slid forward. "I didn't mean it."

Ana sat on the toilet seat and continued to stroke Janae's head. "You should have been more careful with your words."

Janae pulled away from Ana and stood. "They were just words. Nobody heard me."

Ana stood. "Oh, but they are heard and accounted for in heaven."

Clenching her fists, Janae paced the bathroom. "This isn't normal. People have said worse things and don't get sucked into this hell of a..." What was she in?

"Hell?" Ana put her hands on Janae's shoulders, stopping her movement.

"Lots of people have divorced and not ended up like this."

Mr. Chang banged on the door. "You okay? Who in there with you?"

Janae hollered back. "No one. I'm just talking to myself."

"Finish conversation and get back to work."

Once again, Ana had vanished. Janae splashed cold water on her face and dried any residue of sorrow.

With trembling hands, she scrolled through her contacts, stopping when she reached Claire. She didn't even know what to say to her. "Congratulations for stealing him away from me, for adding one more stab wound to my already broken heart."

In the end, she tucked the phone back in her pocket.

The mirror reflected back someone even more miserable than the poor souls who came through the store doors.

Mr. Chang waited for her at the register helping an elderly man make a purchase of a cheap necklace. Janae's stomach lurched. Had he already discovered the missing money?

Keeping her words light, Janae said, "I'll take over for you."

Mr. Chang stepped aside and whispered, "You look like you have velly bad day."

"Not any worse than yesterday." Which held more truth than she wanted to share.

Customers kept her so busy that Janae didn't have time to reflect on the afternoon, nor to put the money back. Tonight, she'd crawl into bed and have her pity party. First, she'd slip several treats in her purse on the way out the door and wallow in as many gummy bears as she could. What did it matter what she stole? It would all be back the way it was the day before, or the week, or year, or the rest of her pitiful life. The twenty-dollar bill seemed to burn her through the pocket.

No, she couldn't do that to the Changs. They worked hard to provide a meager living for themselves and had been more than generous in offering her a job when no one else would.

She opened the drawer, pulled the money from her pocket, eyed it for moment, then put her hand into the till.

"Ah, ha!" Mrs. Chang shouted. "I knew you no good for store."

Mr. Chang came to the counter. "What you mean, wife?"

Mrs. Chang shook her finger at Janae. "I see her steal money from drawer."

Janae's face felt flushed and drained at the same time. "No, please, it's not like that." How could she tell them that she *had* taken it and then had realized that she should never have taken it in the first place?

"Is this true? You take from hand to feed you?" Mr. Chang asked, disbelief on his face.

Janae hung her head. "I'm sorry." She prayed they would be understanding. "I just don't have enough to get me through the week."

"You steal from boss?" Mr. Chang pulled his eyebrows together as if he didn't believe her.

Her shoulders hung as if her arms would slide off and fall to the floor. "I'll get my purse."

Neither of the Changs said anything to her when she left the counter and went to the office. When Janae returned, they were arguing in Chinese. She suspected it had to do with her. Avoiding eye contact, she slipped out the door and went into the shoe repair shop next door.

The merchant looked up and studied Janae as if she was the one who was indigent. "Can I help you?"

"No." She sat on the stool beside the window. "I forgot my coat, and I'm just waiting for the tram."

He set the hammer in his hand down on the counter. "Don't steal anything."

Until today, she'd never dreamed she'd stoop that low. "I won't; I promise."

He didn't move from the counter, continuing to eye her as if she really was a common thief.

The tram pulled up to the station. If she didn't step up her pace, she'd miss it and have to wait out in the cold for the next one. Dreading the walk home in the dark, she raced across the parking lot and hit that patch of black ice, flinging her backward onto the pavement, slamming her head against the asphalt.

26

January 4, 2010

"Mrs. Williams?" A hand gently shook Janae.

Janae opened her eyes and took a quick glance around the room. Ethan's office was in such a disarray that it left her with no doubt as to where in time she'd awakened. They'd rented space several months ago in this building so that Ethan could move his office out of their home.

Rubbing her temples, Janae glanced up at Kaylee, the older, teen girl Janae hired to take care of Lili. She couldn't stand the thought of leaving her daughter with anyone other than Kayleen. And where better for someone to babysit than right here in Ethan's office.

Kaylee carried Lili on her hip.

She remembered this time in her life. "Hello little miss." Janae held out her arms to take her baby girl, relishing in the moment that her daughter was still alive, and still as precious.

Lili practically flung herself into Janae's arms and tugged at her shirt, wanting to be nursed.

Janae made a half-hearted effort to fight off her daughter, while kissing her under her chin and tickling her neck, hoping to distract her, and yet at the same time, wanting this moment to never end. Janae remembered she'd been trying to ween her for several weeks, and Lili still wouldn't cooperate.

"Lili still keeping you awake at night?" Kaylee asked.

Janae nodded. "You'd think that a one-year-old child could sleep through the night."

Kaylee shrugged. "I suppose." She pointed to the door to the exterior waiting area. Your last interview is here."

"Perfect, thank you." Reluctantly, she handed Lili back to the sitter, pushed some papers aside and took out the applicant's file. Claire. The woman who would try to steal her husband after Lili's death. A knot the size of the desk formed in her stomach.

Janae stiffened at the knock on the door. She dreaded what would happen next. What if she made another mistake? Her mind was muddled, incapable of … Janae breathed out, forcing herself to calm her racing heart. "Come in."

When the door pushed open and admitted Claire, Janae swallowed the knot threatening to strangler her.

"Hello, Mrs. Williams." The blue-eyed, busty, barely-out-of-college blond entered the office with her hand extended.

Janae ignored it and motioned to the chair. "I see that you graduated top of your class in business management."

Claire took the seat opposite Janae. "Yes, ma'am." Her perfectly coiffed hair along with her tailored suit gave off an air of confidence, the very thing that had led Janae to hire her.

"Why would you want to work in a measly construction company as a secretary?" The last thing Janae wanted to do was let this woman take the position and then steal her husband away. The first time she'd hired Claire, she'd been impressed with her credentials. This time, Janae wouldn't let the degree fool her.

"I'd like to get a feel for a small business, and then if this works well, perhaps your company's growth would allow me to move into a managerial position in helping to run the office and manage the accounts." Claire pointed to part of her resume. "As you can see, I've also taken many classes in accounting." She exuded tenacity mingled with her self-assured poise.

Janae knew better than to trust her alone in the office with her husband, even when they hired an in-house bookkeeper and a secretary while Claire took over the position as office manager. That had obviously not been enough chaperoning. "Thank you, Miss Brewer. I'll get back with you in a day or two and let you know what we've decided."

An innocent smile crossed her face and lit up her eyes. "Thank you so much for this opportunity. I just know I will be an asset to your company."

Claire would prove to be a benefit for William's Contracting saving their family hundreds of thousands of dollars. As office manager, she'd run an organized office, hire competent workers, do all the things Janae didn't want to do and more. But at what price? The cost of her marriage? It wasn't worth it.

Janae smiled. "I have several more interviews. I'll let you know tomorrow."

The smile didn't hide the disappointment that fell across her face. "It was nice meeting you." Claire held out her hand. It would be rude not to shake it. Her grip was firm and confident.

Lili's cries from the other room. "You can see yourself out."

Claire nodded and left the room.

Janae had been able to take care of William's Contracting for Ethan once the older kids had started school. Lili hadn't been a problem until now. Janae had had to find a sitter who could watch the baby while Janae helped to run her husband's growing business.

Taking another deep breath, probably the hundredth of the afternoon, Janae unclenched her fists and set Claire's resume at the bottom of the pile.

"Hey, little pumpkin," Claire's voice came through the open door. "Are you hungry?"

Janae hurried into the outer office. "She's fine. It's just her naptime."

Claire tucked her hair behind her ear. "Oh." Her gaze fell on the portable crib set up in the corner. "I'll bet you'll be glad to have help so you can watch your little one at home, huh?"

"Indeed." Janae hadn't meant to sound so abrupt. She took Lili from the sitter and crossed to the crib. "You can go now."

In the awkward silence, Claire's shoulders slumped, and she left the office.

Janae had meant that for Kaylee. It didn't matter anyway, because the last person she would hire was Claire Brewer. She held out Kaylee's weekly pay. "Thank you."

"No problem. Lili's a doll." Kaylee stroked the baby's cheek. "Do you still need me next week?"

Janae laid Lili in her crib. "Yes, and probably the week after that while I train the new secretary."

Kaylee slipped on her jacket. "That last one seemed nice."

"I suppose." Nice was not what Janae needed. Efficient, hardworking, good with numbers as well as people is what Ethan needed to run his office. Claire was all of those things. She was the most qualified for the job, and she would have made a great addition to the company.

"See you on Monday." Kaylee said, then hurried out the door.

As Janae sat at Ethan's desk, the quiet filling the room, she poured over the resumes again. Sorting them into qualification, Claire's kept ending up on the top of the list each time she compared the six candidates.

Several of the carpenters entered the outer office, their voices loud for a moment, and then hushed to whispers. They must have seen Lili still napping. They wouldn't have to tiptoe around once Janae hired a secretary.

"Sorry Mrs. W.," Mike said when he entered the office and set his time sheet on the desk.

Janae looked up at the clock. She'd been sitting here for nearly two hours. "It's all right; Lili should be waking up soon anyway." She took first Mike's then Spencer's. "Give me a minute, and I'll work up your pay."

Lili stirred and stood in her crib. "Mama," she cooed and then fussed.

Mike went into the other room and picked her up. "How about I hold you while your mama pays me." He looked over his shoulder at Janae, "I won't even charge you for babysitting."

Janae smirked. "It's either hold her or wait until Monday." Her eyes burned from lack of sleep, and her stomach growled. She must have missed lunch. She had to hire someone soon. She couldn't keep doing this.

Mike bounced Lili in his arms. "I don't mind at all." He cooed at Lili. "We don't mind at all, do we?" He rubbed her nose with his, and she giggled.

While it was nice that the employees were so kind to Lili, Janae needed to be home with her daughter.

After calculating the deductions, she wrote out their checks, and handed them to Mike and Spencer.

"Thanks." Mike traded Lili for his pay.

"See you Monday." Janae waved as the men left the office.

Janae finally gave up fighting her daughter for possession of her body and nursed Lili until Ethan walked in.

"I thought you were going to ween her." He set his hard hat on the desk.

Janae stroked the baby's soft cheek. "I've tried."

"How went the interviews?"

This was the moment of truth. She couldn't hire Claire. "I've interviewed them all, and after careful consideration, I think you should go with Carol Gordon."

Ethan pulled his eyebrows together. "Really? I thought we'd talked about Claire Brewer when we saw her resume."

How did she explain that she knew what would happen? She couldn't keep using knowing the future, could she? "I know she looks good on paper, but after speaking with her, I just don't think she's right for what you need." And definitely not right for what their marriage needed.

Ethan leaned over and kissed her forehead. "If you think Carol is what we need, then let's do it."

27

Later that evening, Janae tucked Lili into bed later than usual. Her other children were spending the night at Gina's house for a Grammy day camp tomorrow with the other older cousins. All ten of her grandchildren looked forward to this monthly sleepover. Janae had no idea how her mother-in-law handled them all when she could barely manage four of her own.

Exhausted from nursing, nursing, and then nursing again, Janae trudged down the hall and fell into bed. She should tackle the laundry, or sort through some toys, at least take a quick shower. Even that seemed like too much energy. Would it matter one night that she didn't brush her teeth or put on pajamas?

Ethan crawled into bed beside her. "Kind of quiet tonight?" He always looked forward to this time alone with her.

Tonight, she was just too tired. "I swear, tomorrow, I'm not giving in to her." Except what would happen tomorrow?

"She's our last." He stroked the hair off her forehead.

Ethan was right. Lili was her last. Janae let out a sigh of contentment. All of her children were well, happy…and most important…alive. She'd had this day with all of them. She'd averted the destruction of her marriage. For today, even if she woke up tomorrow in that same stupid, ugly dilapidated apartment, she'd treasure today. Forever.

Janae rolled over to face the man she adored. "I love you."

His kisses fluttered across her cheek, down her neck, until her phone rang. "Can't we ever get some alone time?" he grumbled.

She reached back to retrieve her phone off the nightstand.

Ethan grabbed her hand before she got ahold of it. "Ignore it."

Her heart started pounding. Grace. She just knew it had something to do with her daughter. "I have to answer it." Janae squirmed out of Ethan's hold and answered the phone.

Gina's voice on the other. "It's Grace."

Fear shook her insides before she passed out.

28

Saturday, November 22, 1997

Janae didn't want to wake, didn't want to face the tragedy of today. Grace was her last living child. Would today be the day she lost her daughter as well? How could she go on without her precious girl? "I hate you, Ana!" she yelled into the darkness of her room.

This was new. The last several times, Janae had awakened to light pouring through the window. Peeking through one eye, she examined her surroundings. From the light in the hallway, the damask wallpaper looked darker above the blue wainscoting. This was her old room before Mom had redecorated it.

She jumped out of bed, flipped on the switch, and checked her face in the mirror. No wrinkles, her hair in a flipped-out bob, well it would be after she blew it dry and styled it. What day was it? She searched her purse for her phone and came up empty-handed. Was she still in high school? Or was this her college years? They all kind of blended together.

This! She could fix everything...all of her children. If she was still living at home, she... Janae knew exactly what she had to do.

Down the hall, in the kitchen her mother hung a calendar. Not that Mom ever crossed off days or wrote down events. At least Janae would know the month and year.

November. Turning the calendar over, she read the year. She ran her hand over the page. Mom had circled Thanksgiving and written 2 PM at Grandma's house. That helped some. Did they already attend dinner with all the aunts and uncles and cousins?

Mom padded down the hall and stopped in front of where Janae stood holding the calendar. Her hair was as blond as she remembered when Mom was younger. The Bailey resemblance ran strong in their family. They must have gotten it from Great-grandma Ana. "You're not sleeping in?" Mom asked.

Janae scratched her head. "I think I lost a day. I may have even lost a whole month. What's the date today?"

Mom pointed to the box on the calendar. "November twenty-second."

"Saturday." Janae could think of no reason this day was special.

"Are you still planning on going with us to Grandma's house?" Mom went to the fridge and pulled out the milk.

"Why wouldn't I?" Janae asked.

"I just wondered if you'd decided to go to Ethan's house this year."

Janae slumped down into the chair. She suddenly remembered exactly which day this was. Butterflies flurried around her stomach like they might burst through. "Ethan's going to propose to me."

"What?" Her mother set the milk on the counter. "He is?"

"Uh, I hope so." Janae carried inside her all the love she'd had for her boyfriend back then. They'd met at the student union. He had been flirting with some pretty girl with chestnut hair as they sat close to the double doors. He was tall and oh, so handsome, but not quite as buff as he was after he'd worked years in construction.

Janae's eyes had met his, and for a moment she could have sworn "I love you" formed on his lips. He must have been saying them to the other girl.

Janae had turned to go to the cafeteria, but the guy's motions caught her attention.

Ethan then patted the girl's hand and excused himself. She hadn't look irritated at all, and that puzzled Janae. In long strides, he'd caught up to her. "Don't I know you?"

That was the lamest pick-up line she'd ever heard. "I don't think so."

"No, I'm sure we've met somewhere before."

Janae chuckled. "Do you always hit on girls this way? Why don't you go back to Miss Brunette? She looks more your type."

Ethan laughed. "That's my sister."

Blinking, Janae took a closer look at the girl. "Sister, huh?" They did look similar, even their hair coloring and drop-dead gorgeous smile.

"Then you know she's not my type." Ethan held out his hand. "Ethan Williams. And you're..."

"Janae Bailey."

"I thought I knew you!" The excitement had surrounded him, exuding as much effervescence as his spicy cologne. She breathed in his manly scent, her heart beating wildly in her chest.

"Hello, Earth to Janae." Mom's words brought her out of her memory. "How do you know he's proposing? You've only been dating for a couple of months."

A smile crept up her face and the butterflies ramped up their pace. "A girl just kind of knows these things." She practically floated down the hall to the bathroom.

Ethan was supposed to be picking her up for a sunrise breakfast. He'd bring her raspberry hot chocolate, which had become her favorite, because it was his favorite. Then he was taking her back to his dorm. Only she was supposed to have no idea what he'd planned.

Since she changed her hair style, blowing it dry was easy-peasy. Dressed in her black jeans, boots and her favorite turquoise shirt, she applied her makeup with extra care.

The soft knock on the bathroom door surprised her. "Ethan's here!" Mom sounded as excited as Janae.

"Tell him I'll be right there." A few spritzes of his favorite floral perfume and he'd find her irresistible.

When she met Ethan in the living room, he held two Styrofoam coffee cups, hot chocolate wafting through the air.

"Hey beautiful." He handed her one of the cups. "You ready?"

Containing herself until he got down on one knee was going to prove nearly impossible. "Hold this." She handed the cup back to him, grabbed her coat and scarf and caught a quick glimpse of her mother standing down the hallway. A smile spread across her face. She was glad her parents approved of Ethan. Was it his rugged good looks or the fact that an engineering degree promised the world on a platter for their youngest daughter? He would become her whole world, her forever companion.

When they got close to his student housing, he stopped the car, leaned over, and held out a scarf. "Cover your eyes."

"Okay?" She had to pretend to be surprised even though she knew what was coming next. With the scarf over her face, Ethan eased the car up the road. Once he parked, he opened his door. "Stay right there; I'll come around and get you."

The butterflies in her stomach suddenly turned to angry bees. Something wasn't sitting right. She swallowed when he opened the door and took her hand, drawing her from the car. With his arm tightly gripped around her shoulder, he led her. "Step up."

She lifted her foot and felt the curb below her boots.

Ethan released his arm from around her, took both her hands and pulled her forward. Then he let go. "You can take off the blindfold now."

Her heart raced as the bees traversed her insides. This was it, the moment she said yes.

In the leaves scattering the front lawn, Ethan had raked out a message. "Will you marry me?" He knelt on the sidewalk holding out an open box with a ring inside the blue velvet lining.

As if the bees had escaped and raced around her in a cloud of confusion, they formed the image of Grace's face. Distant, fleeting, Janae tried to reach out to her. What had happened with Grace when Gina called?

More than a dozen college students stood on the sidewalk. Cameron, Ethan's best friend held a camera and shouted, "Say yes, you crazy woman."

Crazy?

She couldn't say yes; she had to say no for Liliana, for Taylor, for Ryan and for Grace. "I can't."

29

Ethan arose as if the agony from her rejection had fallen into his knees. He closed the ring box and tucked it in his pocket. "Why?"

That single question transferred all his hurt to Janae's heart. "You wouldn't understand."

He took her hands, holding them like they were made of frost, and she'd dissipate into thin air if he held too tightly. "Help me understand."

Janae closed her eyes to avoid the pain in his. "You wouldn't believe me if I told you."

His thumbs brushed across the back of her hands. "Is it too soon in our relationship? Should I have waited, dated longer? Was I mistaken when you said you loved me?"

The sensation of his touch transferred every bit of misery to Janae. Of course, she loved him. Breaking up with him now would save her children. "Ethan... I... can't explain it."

"Well, you owe me an explanation." Hurt and irritation hung on his words.

She was insane not to marry him. He was crazy-passionate about everything. They would have a wonderful, though imperfect life...until they lost Liliana. Then everything would fall apart—her sanity, her marriage... everything. It would be better if she never had a husband, children... a life. If she remained a spinster, her children would never be born and then they'd never have to die. Yet how could she explain all this to Ethan.

He released her hands and pulled her into his arms. The warmth of his breath on her cheek made it impossible to think. How had she fallen so helplessly in love with him in such a short time? "Please help me understand," he whispered in her ear.

All she wanted to do was melt into him. The beating of his heart passed through his jacket, through her own, the sorrow of a lifetime echoed against her. She loved the way he held her. She felt cherished, protected in his arms. If he held her like this forever, all could be right with the world, couldn't it? It was the "could be" that terrified her.

The wind swirled around them, rearranging the proposal on the ground into an indiscernible pattern.

Janae pushed him away. "I need to go home."

"You still haven't told me why you can't marry me." Were those tears choking his words?

Didn't she owe him some kind of explanation? Yes, she did, but not here in front of an audience.

His best friend still had the camera pointed at them. "Come on, Janae, just say yes."

Ethan signaled for Cameron to stop recording, then led Janae to his car.

They sat in silence for so long, Janae wondered who would break the silence first. After a while, he pulled into a parking lot. His hands hadn't left the steering wheel and his knuckles had grown white where he gripped it.

"Ethan, you don't want me. I'm a damned soul."

He released his hold on the steering wheel and turned to face her. "I would follow you to Hell just to be with you."

How close he was to the truth and didn't realize it. She picked up the paper mug she'd left in the car earlier and rolled it between her fingers. Focusing on the motion, she wouldn't have to look into Ethan's devastated eyes. "If we get married, horrible things will happen."

"All marriages go through some rough times." He reached out to still her hands. "But together we can face whatever challenges life throws at us."

Finally daring to look up at him, she had to choke back the tears threatening to burst free. Why couldn't she have still felt this love for him after Liliana drowned? "You don't know where I've been. I've seen our future. We don't make it. Our children won't survive."

He took the cup from her and put it back in the center console, then held onto her hands. "That doesn't make any sense."

Did she dare tell him what she knew would happen? "Would you believe me if I told you I've seen our future firsthand, that I witness the deaths of our children?"

"Did you have a nightmare?"

Janae shuddered and tried to pull away from him. "You get to wake up from a nightmare. I keep reliving parts of our future, only the parts that were good, turn out bad, horrific."

"Explain to me what happened." Ethan kept a firm hold on her as if she'd disappear, which she knew could happen the minute she closed her eyes.

He would think she was crazy and then not want to marry her after all. Maybe it was best to tell him everything. "I wake up every morning and it's in the future...over 20 years from today."

"And we live in a tiny house filled with children."

How could she tell him about the last words she'd whispered before this whole nightmare happened? If only she could just wake up. No, everything she experienced was real. She shook her head. "No, I live in a studio apartment because we're divorced. You still live in our beautiful home."

He brought his hand to her neck and drew her closer. "I would never divorce you."

"But I would you." She swallowed the regret fighting its way to her throat.

"Why would you do that when we're so crazy in love?"

His fingers in her hair at the base of her neck was making it hard for her to think. "Because you let our daughter drown."

Ethan's hand dropped into his lap, and he stared out the front window. "What if I promise you right now that I will do everything in my power to protect her?"

Janae's heart leapt into her throat, the beat racing as the tears threatening to fall. "Do you promise?"

"With all my heart." He looked back up at her; the intensity in his eyes caught her off guard.

She backed away. "Then you believe me?"

"Sweetheart, if you had some kind of vision that is warning us about the future, then I will do whatever it takes to keep us safe."

Could she believe him? He'd never lied to her in their seventeen years of marriage, until Liliana's death. Would warning him be enough to prevent the horrible events of the future? "You promise that no matter what, no matter how painful the truth might be, you'll always, and I mean always be honest with me?"

He nodded and took her hands again, hope springing to his face. "I promise."

"Then yes, I'll marry you." Janae threw her arms around him.

30

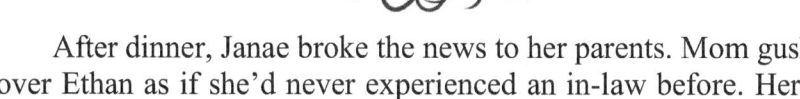

After dinner, Janae broke the news to her parents. Mom gushed all over Ethan as if she'd never experienced an in-law before. Her father scowled, exactly the same way he'd done when her sisters had announced their engagements.

Mom patted Ethan's hand. "Don't let Mr. Grumpy scare you off."

Ethan's smile never left his face, nor did his hand wander far from Janae's. She liked the way he felt, his grip firm, but tender. She wondered if he thought she might vanish. Did she dare believe that perhaps, possibly, just maybe she could stay in this time? Would Ethan really be able to change the events of the future? Wouldn't it be his job to protect his family? They could start fresh, not make so many mistakes like they'd done, or would do in the future. Was it fair to know the future? It could serve as a warning, couldn't it?

Mom and Dad left the room, allowing the "love-birds" to set a date for the wedding. Mom had already told them which dates were a no-go. Now they just needed to figure out how to squeeze in getting married in the middle of the semester. Christmas break was too soon and neither of them wanted to wait until after the spring one.

Janae pulled her bulky planner out of her purse and opened to November. "Thanksgiving with my family and Christmas with yours."

"You'd give up Christmas with all your nieces and nephews?" Ethan cuddled closer to her on the couch.

A smile crept up her face. "You have no idea what a big deal Thanksgiving is to my family. My mom made my sibs promise that it was the one holiday that no matter how far away they moved, they'd always come home for Thanksgiving."

"But what about Christmas?" he asked.

Janae could see why that one day a year would be a big deal for him since his siblings still lived at home. "My parents travel during the Christmas holiday. I usually go with them." She ran her hand across his jawline, loving the slight stubble forming. "But not this year."

"Won't they be upset?"

"Are you kidding?" She chuckled. "A son-in-law in exchange for refunding my ticket to Japan. Seems like a pretty good trade to me."

"I like the way that sounds, Miss Bailey, soon to be Mrs. Williams." Ethan set the calendar behind him and drew her close to him, tilting her chin up. Their eyes met before Janae closed hers and his mouth descended to kiss her. His lips warm and gentle on hers sent her insides tingling.

She wrapped her arms around his neck and pulled him into a deeper kiss. Breathless she pulled away. "I could spend forever right here with you."

"Let's get married after your parents get back from their Christmas holiday. How about a New Year's wedding?" He traced the line of her jaw before dropping his hand to the hollow of her neck.

The familiar sensations of wanting him raced through her veins. "Let's elope right now."

His hand moved to her waist and brought her closer. "My mom would kill me. I guess that's the curse of being the oldest."

"Then New Year's it is." She melted into him; the stroking of his fingers in her hair soothed her. A yawn escaped. "I hope my mother doesn't mind too much with such short notice. Maybe she'll have to refund all three tickets. My sister will understand."

"I love you," Ethan whispered into her ear.

She tucked her head under his chin with her ear over his heart, the rhythm steady and strong. "I love you, too, Mr. Williams."

31

Friday, December 13, 2019

Janae hadn't meant to fall asleep in Ethan's arms, but she couldn't think of a more contented place to be. Snuggling into his chest, he lost his firmness and felt more like...a pillow?

"Wake up sunshine, you're going to be late for work!"

Janae moaned and rolled over. "No, I fixed things." She wasn't supposed to flash forward in time again.

"You don't have time for a shower, so just put your hair up in a ponytail." Ana pulled the black pants and blue shirt from the closet.

If Ethan had promised, then why was she back here in this stupid, abysmal, dingy, ugly, ramshackle... Janae ran out of words to describe her circumstance.

"You only have thirty minutes, so I suggest you hurry." Ana popped two slices of bread into the toaster.

"I'm not hungry." Janae picked up her phone on her nightstand and scrolled down to Grace's contact information. With a sigh of relief her daughter was still there.

"Grace, honey..."

"Mom?"

"Yes, listen to me; I have to tell you something really important."

"O...kay..."

Janae couldn't let the day go by without telling Grace how important she was to her. "I love you. No matter what happens in the past,

I'll do everything I can to protect you."

Irritation hung thick in her words. "Have you been drinking? Did you remember to take your meds?"

Janae held the phone to her ear as if the motion would bring Grace closer to her. "No, but I just wanted you to know before I can't tell you anymore."

Panic rose in Grace's voice. "You're not going to kill yourself because of what happened, are you?"

"No, of course not!" Why would Grace even think such a thing?

"Well, don't."

"And when you talk to your dad, tell him I'm sorry about everything and I know about Claire. I forgive him for that, too. Just ask him to call me, okay?"

"What are you talking about? Dad's been gone for four years."

A slug in the stomach couldn't have stolen her breath like this. "What do you mean, gone?"

"As in all the stress you caused him. You should remember."

Janae shook her head trying to rid the words she'd just heard. "No, I would never have hurt your father."

"You just as well have killed him."

"No, Grace, I didn't."

Her exasperated huff came through the phone. "You're right, you didn't pull the trigger, but you just as well have."

The line went dead.

The phone dropped to the floor as Janae searched for Ana. "Ethan's...dead?"

Sorrow filled Ana's eyes. "Heart attack."

"Why?" Janae's hands trembled. Did she want to know the answer?

Ana slumped down onto the bed beside her. "When you left him after Lili's death, his heart broke. He promised to protect his family, he wasn't able, and then you left him." She put her hand on Janae's. "He couldn't go on without you."

Her heart slammed against her ribs so hard she thought it might burst through the bones. "He was so strong and healthy." How could this have happened? "I loved Ethan. He was everything to me."

Hadn't he just kissed her last night, held her in his arms, promised ... He promised, and now he was gone.

She turned from Ana pulling her hands from her. "Go away." Then she curled into a ball, sobbing.

Her phone rang, she ignored it. The toast popped up from the toaster. She didn't care. When the neighbor upstairs started banging around, she tried to shut out the sound with her pillow over her ears. She envied the woman who danced around her apartment as if no one was watching her. There was no one left for Janae.

How could she go on? What meaning was life without Ethan?

"Let me go back," She whispered when the night grew dark and quiet. Except she had no idea where in her life she could fix it. Not only had it not helped, she'd made it worse. And yet how could she go on with her empty, pitiful life? What if she just joined her family in death?

Janae went to the medicine cabinet and stopped in front of the mirrored door. Where had those dark circles come from? Gone was the happiness from her eyes. She opened the door and looked at the medications piled inside. Some of them prescription—antidepressants, some found in any cabinet, aspirin, ibuprofen, Tylenol. Who would find her? Grace? Probably not. Was there anyone left who cared about Janae?

Her hand hovered over the bottle of aspirin. How many should she take?

Someone knocked on the door.

Ignore it?

Like the phone?

The toaster?

The neighbor?

"Janae?"

Gina.

She ignored her, too.

"Janae, are you there?"

No, she wasn't here. Not anymore.

Janae uncapped the bottle and dumped out a handful of pills.

The pounding on the door increased. "Janae Bailey, you open this door now!"

Janae continued to ignore her mother-in-law. She went to the cupboard, got a glass, and filled it with tap water. First one pill, followed by another and another. She stopped counting after...

The door banged opened and her mother-in-law rushed to her side. "What is going on?"

"Nothing." Janae dumped the remaining pills back into the bottle. "I have a headache is all." She turned to the door and spotted Ana disappearing outside. Did Ana open the door? Why had she tried to save Janae?

Gina took the bottle from Janae. "How many did you take?"

"I don't know...maybe two or three, I guess." Actually, it had been closer to five or six; she didn't want to tell her.

"You're coming home with me right now." Gina didn't wait for her to pack anything but dragged her out of the house and down the sidewalk where Grace sat in the front seat of her mother-in-law's car.

Janae hesitated on the sidewalk, pulling out of her mother-in-law's grip. "What's Grace doing here?" How could she let her only daughter see the horrid state she was in?

Gina grabbed Janae's arm again and forced her to the car. "Grace was worried about you. She said you wouldn't answer your phone. And then I tried calling you. Your boss said you never showed up at work today."

Numb, Janae couldn't speak, couldn't argue, couldn't do anything, so she allowed her mother to shove her into the backseat of the car.

Grace turned around. "Mom, are you alright?"

No, she wasn't. She never would be. If only she could melt into the floorboards and cease to exist.

"What happened?" Graced turned and asked Mom.

"I think she's taken too many aspirin."

"Can you overdose on them?"

"I don't know." Gina put the bottle in Grace's hand.

"How many did she take?"

"Not many, I think. If I hadn't stopped her..." Gina let the words trail off.

They talked about Janae as if she wasn't there.

Then it happened again. Only this time, Gina ran the red light and a truck barreled into them.

"Not my Grace!" Janae screamed.

32

---~⟨∞⟩~---

Thursday, January 1, 1998

"Janae. Janae?" Mom's words floated to her as if she was far away on a cloud, white puffs surrounding her face.

"Janae, honey, your mother's talking to you." Her father's voice broke through the fog. She flung her arms around him. "You're here." She wanted to sob into his... tuxedo? Why was he wearing formal wear?

Dad tucked Janae's hand into the crook of his arm. "Of course, I'm here. Where else would I be on the most important day of my daughter's life?"

She pulled away. Mom's dress? Janae recognized the fabric, black paisley Jacquard with the red shrug. Then all this white fluff was her wedding gown. She'd gone back in time to her own wedding. The day her blissful life with Ethan began. Except in the future, Janae knew better.

If she could stop this from happening, she and Ethan wouldn't have children. None of them would be born and she wouldn't have to suffer the agony of losing them. How could she face her life without them? Should she remain single forever and never know the love of her family?

Mom fluffed the veil and patted Janae's shoulders. "I always dreamed your wedding would be this beautiful."

Dad chuckled. "You've said this about all your girls."

The music from the other room swelled. "I guess I should get to my seat." Mom lifted the veil and gave Janae a quick kiss on the cheek. "Why are you shaking? You've been looking forward to this day since Ethan proposed."

The proposal. Janae had made him promise to protect their children. Even if she lost her kids, she couldn't let Ethan take the blame. "I can't do this."

"Take a deep breath. It's just cold feet." Mom patted her hand. "Your amazing guy is out there waiting for you." Mom took a moment to look at Janae.

Why couldn't Mom read the fear behind Janae's eyes.? Mom turned and went into the chapel, leaving Janae alone with her father. If she told *him* about the future, would he believe her? Would he make her go through with her marriage?

"Dad, I..." She looked into his beaming eyes, so full of love and hope for his youngest daughter.

"It's natural to get cold feet." He patted her head like he'd done when she was little and needed his comfort.

Janae put her hand on his arm. "This isn't just cold feet. What if things go wrong? What if everybody I love dies?"

A soft smile crinkled his crow's feet. "Sweetheart, we don't know what the future holds. Every couple has their ups and downs."

"What if I've seen the future, and everything turns out horrible? What if Ethan and I don't make it?"

He tucked her hand once more into the crook of his arm and with his other hand, pulled her into an embrace. "If you ever feel like you are so angry with him that you want to leave, remember the promises you'll make in just a few minutes." His expression turned more serious than she'd ever seen. "And never, ever, under any circumstances mention the word divorce, not in passing, not in jest. Many couples' marriages could have been saved if they'd stayed and fought for the love they had. It's going to get messy and ugly at times, but I promise, if you stand by your commitment today, then you'll make it."

He thought he was giving her the best possible fatherly advice. But he hadn't seen what she had.

The wedding march swelled through the door. "Well, precious, that's our cue." He didn't wait for her to answer as he opened the door and guided her into the chapel.

So many familiar faces beamed at her. They didn't know what she knew, or they would have told her to run. Her stomach sank to her feet when Ethan's gaze caught hers. His smile reached across his face. Had he ever looked so handsome, or so much in love with her? If she ran now, she could save his life. But what about the lives of their children? In this moment in time, would he remember the promise he'd made to her about protecting their children? Then when he failed would his life be cut short because she broke his heart?

Now more than ever she wanted to take back the words she'd thrown out into the universe. She didn't want to be divorced from him, even though Lili would never be part of their lives. Her heart beat faster and faster as she drew near to him. Could she tell him she changed her mind and didn't want to marry him after all?

Janae closed her eyes and said a quick prayer. "What should I do?" she whispered, hoping that God would hear her and rescue her from this hell she was living.

Dad released her hand to Ethan's outstretched one. The feel of his skin against hers did nothing to calm her. In fact, his touch unsettled hers. *If you love something let it go.* Staring into his eyes, she desperately loved him. How could she have whispered wanting to divorce him so long ago? Time stood still. The officiator's words froze, the people around her didn't move. Ethan's smile sat motionless on his face.

Janae turned to where her mother sat next to her sister, both with tears hanging from their lashes. The baby on her sister's lap had her thumb stuck in her mouth. The audience focused on Janae. This was her day. It had been all about her. Her stomach clenched, and she pulled her hand from Ethan's.

The officiator coughed. "Janae, are you alright?"

Janae nodded, and then shook her head. "I can't marry you, Ethan." She took a step away from him and raced down the aisle toward the doors.

If her heels would have permitted it, she'd have sprinted as far away as she could, as it was, she only reached the vestibule.

Ethan caught up to her and grabbed her hand, spinning her to face him. "I promised you I'd protect our children. Please trust me."

A sob caught in Janae's throat and she released it with a wail. "I can't have you die, too."

Gathering her in his arms, he held her against him. "You've seen more of our future?"

Nodding, the tears soaked his tuxedo. "You didn't save them." Her knees grew weak and she sunk to the floor.

Ethan caught her in his arms, carried her to the nearby couch, and set her on his lap. The hold he had on her wouldn't let her vanish if she'd wanted to. "What can I do? Help me figure out how I can save them."

Janae buried her face in his chest. "Don't marry me."

He reached under her veil and brushed away her tears. "How will that save them?"

"Because they'll never have to be born."

"That's not saving them. That's eliminating them altogether."

A sob forced its way to her throat. "I can't, Ethan. I just can't."

He held her for so long without saying anything, Janae wondered if he was considering his life without her. Her heart longed for him to disagree.

Mom entered the vestibule. "What is going on?"

Dad's voice followed behind her. "Sweetheart, we can't start the wedding without the bride."

Janae didn't dare look up at them. Mom would be thinking about the embarrassment of what she'd done, and Dad would be thinking about the money he lost by her running away at the altar.

Ethan shook his head; she knew because she felt his chin brush across the top of hers.

After a moment, Dad's voice boomed through the microphone. "Looks like our daughter may have cold feet. Ethan's trying to warm them up."

Laughter accompanied his words. He'd always been good at turning a dismal situation around. The doors closed, muffling the rest of his words.

Ethan put his hand under Janae's chin until her face was level with his. With the other hand he pushed the veil back. Written in his eyes was all the despair of a broken man. If he only knew how broken he would become. He took his handkerchief from his pocket and held it out to her.

Janae dabbed her eyes, but it did little to abate her sorrow. "Because you didn't keep your promise, we still lost our children, and you will die of a broken heart. This is the only way I can fix it."

"That's crazy talk."

How could Janae make him see that it was better this way? "It's where I've been. What I've seen."

"You would give up on us and our future children because you're scared?"

"I'm terrified. I would rather let you go than—"

"Risk our happiness?" Ethan interrupted.

Janae pushed herself off his lap. "How can you say that? Losing our children, being divorced, and dying of a heart attack? That's not happiness."

Ethan tried to step in front of Janae. She side-stepped him and walked in the other direction toward the outer doors. "Let me go, Ethan. Don't you see it's for the best?"

He didn't try to stop her when she left the church and walked toward the bus stop. How she wished he'd come running after her and tell her it didn't matter because he loved her. That he would do all in his power to stop the horrible events.

He didn't.

Janae got off the bus a block away from her house, went upstairs, took off her dress and veil, and curled into a ball on her bed.

Not more than a few minutes later a soft knock sounded on her bedroom door.

When she didn't answer, the door flung open. "Well, this is a fine mess you've gotten yourself into." A woman stood in the light coming from the hall with her hands on her hips.

"Ana?" Janae sat up. Her guardian angel had never shown up in the past. "What are you doing here?"

She entered the room and stood at the foot of the bed. "Ethan doesn't deserve to be left at the altar like that."

"He doesn't deserve to die, and he certainly doesn't deserve the misery I'm going to bring into his life."

"That man loves you with all his heart."

Angry, Janae stood and crossed the short space to stand nose to nose with Ana. "Then why didn't he come after me?"

"Because he's back at the chapel asking your friends and family to pray for you." Did Janae detect a note of irritation in Ana's voice?

"Why would he do that?" Janae asked.

"Because that boy is crazy for you." Ana took Janae's hand and glared into her eyes. "Do you love him?"

"More than life." Janae wondered how her heart managed to be beating with the abuse it had taken in the last ten years, twenty years. Or was it only days?

"Then let's get you back to the chapel." Ana wrapped her hands around Janae's shoulder.

A swirling mist gathered around her, white like her veil, soft like the satin in her dress before blacking out.

33

Friday, December 13, 2019

Janae opened her eyes expecting to find herself at the chapel. Instead she was back in her dingy apartment with its tainted windows letting in the dirtiest of light.

Ana was nowhere to be seen and her black pants and blue shirt lay at the foot of her bed.

"Yeah, yeah, I know, I'm going to be late if I don't get dressed."

The apartment seemed unusually quiet. The neighbor upstairs hadn't started her dance routine. The light coming through the window said morning, about the time she should be getting up. "Ana?"

Ana didn't answer.

In the bathroom, she splashed cold water on her face, then studied herself in the mirror. Something about her had changed; the green in her eyes muted, more olive, the bags under her eyes, more defined. Janae had never felt so tired, even after her bout of post-partum exhaustion.

What had happened to her family since she'd left the altar? She scrolled through her contacts. No Grace or Taylor or Ryan, and certainly no Lili. That meant she was no longer divorced because she'd never married Ethan. What had happened since she left Ethan at the altar?

The tears she thought she'd managed to cry out flowed afresh. What a miserable life.

The phone rang.

Work.

"Why you no come on time?" Mr. Chang sounded irritated.

"I'm sorry, I'll be right there." Janae hung up. So much for a quick shower.

When she stepped outside, she searched for Grace's Honda. The only vehicle in front of her apartment was an old, beat-up Toyota Carolla, just like the one she'd had in college. On closer inspection, it was her car. She'd loved that vehicle but hadn't minded when Ethan up-traded it for a new one.

Of course, not being married to Ethan...ever...had altered things.

Janae put the key in the ignition, and it started right up. That was the only thing positive she could think of to come out of her trip to the past. Before heading into work, she dialed her mother.

"Hi sweetheart, what's up?" What a relief to hear her voice.

But Janae didn't want pleasantries; she needed answers. "I need to ask you a couple of questions, and please don't think I've gone crazy."

"Of course not, dear." Mom sounded surprised to hear her voice.

Janae took a deep breath. "What happened to Ethan after I left him at the altar?"

"Why are you bringing that up now?" Mom asked.

"Did I ever marry anyone else?"

"You *are* crazy." The way Mom said it made it sound like she was joking, but Janae knew differently.

"I need you to tell me what my life has been like since that day. Pretend I have amnesia, okay?"

"I suppose that bump on your head has caused you to do some bizarre things."

Janae gripped the steering wheel. "What bump?"

"Right after you broke up with Ethan." Mom paused. "I guess you wouldn't remember the accident."

"Tell me about it. What happened?" Maybe that would explain why she felt like she was going insane.

"You were going down the stairs at school, and you slipped and fell a full flight of stairs."

"So, I've had amnesia all this time?" Now she was getting to the root of her problem. She'd had a traumatic brain injury. Finally, things were starting to make sense.

"No, you've remembered almost everything. Why aren't you remembering now?" Mom asked.

Rounding the corner, Janae pulled into the parking lot. "I don't know. I just need to figure out some things. Did I ever marry?"

"Are you kidding? After your accident, you changed into a completely different person."

"Did I date?"

"Yes, a lot of nice men that would have made you happy, but you sabotaged every relationship you've ever been in." Irritation crept into her voice. "Are you seeing anyone now?"

"Apparently not." Janae put her car in park and stepped out onto the icy ground. "I'm at work now, so maybe I can call you later?"

"Sure, whatever is fine." Although it didn't sound fine.

Once she entered the warm store, she went to the back room and put on her apron.

Mr. Chang was busy dusting shelves and stocking more Christmas items.

"Would you like me to do that?"

"No, you wait on customers." He waved his feather duster toward the front of the store.

A young mother with one child on her hip and another being held by her hand entered the store. Janae remembered the woman, worn, tired, and her husband in a half-way house.

"Can I help you find something for your husband?" Janae asked.

"How did you know I'm shopping for him?" she asked.

"Lucky guess, I suppose."

"My daddy's in jail," the older of the two said.

"I'm sorry to hear that."

"Well, actually he just got released, and he's in a half-way house waiting for probation to allow him to come home." The woman shifted the baby to her other hip.

"Let's see what we can find." Janae repeated the process of taking her up and down several aisles. Once again, the woman checked the prices before settling on a bag of tootsie rolls.

When she left the store, Janae stood at the counter watching her shiver as she made her way to the car.

During her break, Janae wondered if she should call her husband's work. A pang of regret shot through her chest. He'd never been her husband, at least in this weird alternate reality.

She pulled out her phone and opened her Google app, searching for Ethan's construction company. When she couldn't find his business under the name she'd helped him pick out, for his contact information instead. Maybe he'd even moved away. No, his family still lived here. He was probably married with children of his own. She still couldn't find him in the online white pages.

Janae took a deep breath when his name popped up on Facebook. It was him. Her heart fluttered just looking at him. He hadn't changed at all. Though crow's feet crinkled his skin, he was still strong, and handsome, but there was sadness behind his blue eyes. Janae checked his profile. He was in a relationship, but it was complicated it said. He looked to see if there were any pictures of a woman he might be dating. There were a couple of pictures with Claire, but they didn't look intimate. Janae wondered how they'd managed to find each other since he never hired her. But then again, maybe he had. He had a dog but didn't appear to have any children. Her finger hovered over the *Add Friend* button. A pang hit her heart for something that could never be, and she closed out of the app, then went back to work.

Janae spent the rest of her shift helping customers and ringing up their purchases. She pretended this was her life now. At least she'd saved Ethan, though her heart ached for him… and the children who might have been. It was better they hadn't been born and suffered the horrible fates that awaited them. She wondered what would have happened to Grace. Could she have saved her if she'd married Ethan? Could she go back in time so she could hold her again?

Mr. Chang came from the back of the store where he was helping one last customer. Her dirty face and ragged clothes made her look indigent. This was a horrible time of year to be homeless.

He set some packages of gravy mix, instant potatoes, and a can of beef chunks on the counter. "You ring up zero dollars."

Tears filled the woman's eyes. "Please, no. I can pay for

these." She pulled out two quarters and laid them on the counter next to a couple of packages of ramen.

Her boss pushed the quarters back to the woman. "And she take the noodles with her, too."

Janae smiled. So, her boss had a soft spot in his heart after all. Why hadn't she noticed this interaction before? Maybe because Janae had been too anxious to get home.

Janae put the items in a bag and added a couple napkins, a fork, and spoon. As an added thought, to help with the woman's meal, Janae said, "Wait." She raced to the back room and returned with several pieces of tin foil.

"Thank you." The woman stuffed the foil in the bag along with the other items.

"Are you staying in a shelter somewhere?" Janae asked.

She nodded. "It's not far."

"Do you have bus fare?" Janae had no cash on her and hoped the woman said yes.

"I can walk. It's not far."

Janae shivered thinking about being out in the bitter cold without a jacket. "I'm almost done; I can drive you, if you want to wait."

She tucked the bag under her arm. "I'm fine." Then before Janae could argue, the woman left the store and trudged across the parking lot.

"That will be me in a few weeks," Janae said under her breath. "Unless I can find another job."

Mrs. Chang came from the back room, locked the front door, and carried the cash drawer to the office to count the night's take.

"Good night, Mr. Chang." Janae zipped her coat and wrapped her scarf around her neck.

"You be early tomorrow. It's a bigger day."

Two Saturdays before Christmas. Janae nodded. "I'll be here, unless I get sent back in time—again."

"You be on time." Mr. Chang must have missed what she said.

When she opened the outer door, the bitter wind rushed inside, chilling Janae to the core. She could imagine that poor woman trudging to her shelter.

Her thoughts turned to Ana. Why hadn't her great-grandmother shown up today? Maybe because now that she'd more or less straightened out her life, Janae no longer needed a guardian angel.

The car door stuck for a moment before Janae climbed in. When she turned the key, it cranked a couple of times, then went to clicks, and then nothing. "Great!" Grace's car was the one that died like this every night, not her Corolla. She could take the tram if she ran before it left the station. Careful not to slip on the ice she picked her way across the half-salted lot, until she hit that same stupid patch. Her head slammed into the ground and everything went black.

34

Thursday, October 31, 2013

Had Janae frozen to death out there in the parking lot and finally made it to the real Hell?

"Mama, I'm hungwy."

Lili? Janae's eyes flew open and her five-year-old daughter stood in front of her. How could this be? Lili was dead, as were the rest of her children. "What day is it?"

"It's Hawoween."

Janae sat up. She was back in her bedroom and Lili...she was alive! That meant the rest of her children were as well. "How old are you?"

Lili held up three fingers. "I fwee."

This was the day she would lose Taylor...unless...she didn't change anything that morning. That would mean a trip to the ER with Grace. It had been bad, but she'd survived.

"I want some skwambled eggs wiff little pieces of bacon."

Ignoring Lili, Janae flung off the covers and headed for the stairs.

Before she got too far, Ethan blocked her way. "Good morning. I thought you wanted to sleep in today."

Unable to contain herself, she flung her arms around his neck. "You're alive!" The scent of his aftershave enveloped her, and she could have sworn she'd never smelled anything so heavenly.

Ethan pulled her away; an odd smiled crinkled the lines next to his handsome blue eyes. "And hungry." This was the man she'd fallen in love with eons ago when they met at college. "Don't forget the re-pairman is coming over this morning to check on the pool pump."

As she released Ethan, she picked Lili up in her arms. Tears of joy ran down Janae's cheeks. "I've missed you two so much."

Lili pointed to herself. "Silly Mommy, I wight here."

She hugged her tight against her chest, letting the tears flow unabashed. "Yes, you are!"

Ethan shook his head. "You're so emotional, are you expecting a visit from your Aunt Flo?"

Janae chuckled. "You don't get to diagnose that. And I'm not pregnant either." She set her daughter down and took her hand. "Let's get you some breakfast."

Ethan followed her down the stairs. "What has gotten into you?"

Taylor sat at the breakfast bar drinking a glass of juice. "Beth is having a sleep over tonight after the party, can I go?"

"Yes, yes, and yes, you can go." If Taylor went to Beth's she would be fine and come home in the morning. Janae didn't need to do anything to change tonight. It would be tolerable to let the events take their course.

"Thanks, Mom."

Janae went to the kitchen window and stared out into the back-yard. The leaves had scattered across the lawn and floated on the top of the pool, the one Lili would drown in. How could she change that event? If she could fix this part of their lives, maybe it would alter everything else. Fear gripped her stomach. How could she re-turn to that horrible day and prevent what she knew was coming? Why hadn't she returned to *that* day so she could save her Liliana?

Lili climbed onto the barstool next to Taylor. "I come wiff you, too?"

Taylor rolled her eyes. "No babies allowed."

"I not a baby. I fwee years old." Lili held up her fingers again.

Janae ran her finger down her youngest daughter's nose. "You are getting so big. But this party is for older kids."

"I wanna go." Lili flopped onto the counter and wailed.

Janae hated Lili's tantrums... She jerked herself from that train of thought. No, she *used* to hate them. Now they meant Lili was a normal three-year-old, a perfect child with wants and emotions.

Janae picked up Lili and slung her over her shoulder and tickled her sides. "Now, let's get you some breakfast." She set Lili back on the stool.

"Why don't we let Grace take the littles trick-or-treating?" Ethan entered the kitchen, wrapped his arms around her waist, and kissed her. "Then maybe you and I can turn off all the lights and disappear for the evening."

Part of her melted against him. She couldn't remember the last time he'd kissed her like this, her toes curling at his touch and her stomach fluttery like when they were dating.

"As much as I'd love to hang out with you alone, I think you should take the kids. I'll stay here and pass out candy." She trailed her fingers up his chest and wrapped them around Ethan's neck.

He lowered his head, his lips brushing hers with the promise of taking care of unmet desires.

Her stomach tingled. How could she have ever wished to divorce him? That had changed after Lili's death.

Ryan pushed his way around his parents. "Ew, gross, get a room, already." He opened the refrigerator and pulled out the milk.

"Ew, gwoss, get a woom alweady." Except for the three-year-old speech impediment, Lili sounded just like her older brother.

Ethan chuckled. "Don't say anything you don't want her to repeat." He released Janae. "We have a room, in fact a whole house. And if you'd like to pay the mortgage, then you can dictate where I get to kiss your mother."

Grace sat next to Taylor, picked up the carton, and poured herself a glass. "I think it's sweet. I hope my husband isn't ashamed to kiss me any time he wants."

Pushing against his chest, Janae cleared her throat and looked into his blue eyes. These were the good times she remembered.

Lili crawled onto the counter to retrieve the orange juice container.

Janae stepped out of Ethan's embrace and went to the cupboard for a cup. "Here, you can pour it if you want." She set the cup in front of Lili. "I'll hold the cup, and you pour it very carefully."

Ethan stood with his lips pinched together. "Since when do you let her get away with that kind of behavior?"

"She has wants and needs and feelings just like the rest of us." Janae held the cup. "Use both hands."

Obvious shock registered on Ethan's face. "And you're letting her sit on the counter?"

"Her bum isn't going to hurt anything." Janae put the juice back in the fridge before moving Lili back onto the barstool. "I think Daddy prefers that you sit in a chair."

35

As the evening grew closer, Janae's stomach tensed until she thought she was going to throw up. It was all she could do to steady her nerves enough to put on Lili's witch makeup. "Hold still, my little rug rat."

"I want a gween nose wiff a wart, and scary ghost eyes."

"You can have whatever you want." Janae dabbed the green makeup over Lili's face.

Ethan crowded into the downstairs bathroom with them. "Oh, look at my scary goblin."

Lili put her hands on her hips in the way that always made Janae laugh. "I not a goblin, I a witch."

Ethan patted her tummy. "Oh, sorry, Griselda."

Lili folded her arms and turned her nose into the air. "I'm going to get lots of candy."

"I'm sure you will." He snuggled his chin against the back of Janae's neck. "I might get some, too."

Suddenly the room grew ten times smaller, and with Ethan's cologne wafting around her, it made it as many times harder for Janae to think. "After you take Lili and Ryan out, maybe." She pointed to the hall. "You go stand over there. It's too crowded in here with you."

With a look of mock rejection, Ethan left the bathroom, but stood outside, leaning on the door jam.

Ethan took Lili's hand. "Okay you little witchy girl. Let's go scare up some treats." Before he turned down the walk, he put his arm around

Janae's waist and pulled her close. "Keep the home fires burning bright tonight. I might need you to keep the boogie monsters away."

Janae nestled into him. "Since when does a grown man like you need protection?"

His smile lit up his eyes. "I just want to snuggle."

Lili tugged on his hand. "Daddy, let's go!"

Ryan had already headed down the sidewalk. "It's gonna get dark soon."

"I'm coming." Ethan kissed Janae one more time. "That's for the crockpot I started this morning."

"Go." Janae gave him a gentle shove.

She watched them head down the sidewalk for a moment before grabbing her purse and keys. First, she dropped off Taylor. "Have fun."

Grace jumped into the front seat. "You're sure you're okay with it being a boy-girl party?"

"A mother is never ready for that."

"Get used to it." Grace's flippant attitude sent shards of anxiety racing through her veins.

"Just wait until you have a daughter of your own." Janae swallowed the fear. It was just a broken arm. It would mend. Taylor would be safe at Beth's house. Ryan and Lili would each bring home enough candy to compromise their immune systems until Christmas. Again, nothing to worry too much about, yet her stomach continued to twist into knots.

Her family. All of them alive. All of them heading off to an evening of fun. All Janae had to do was wait for the phone call.

After she dropped the girls off, she picked up the candy filled plastic pumpkin and settled into the lawn chair. Within a few minutes costumed trick-or-treaters came up the sidewalk.

"What have we here?" She held out a handful of chocolate minis to an adorable Cinderella and an older vampire.

"I'm Finderella." The little girl held out her bag.

"It's not Finderella, it's Thinderella," the older child said.

The dad standing on the sidewalk chuckled.

A screech of brakes followed by a crash filled the air.

Janae's heart sank to her feet as she sprinted down the street.

"No! This wasn't supposed to happen."

She rounded the corner. There was the teen who'd killed Taylor still sitting in his car. Where was her daughter? "Taylor!" Janae screamed. Something was different. The car's hood was slammed into a light pole and water hissed from the radiator. Blood pooled around his forehead where he'd hit the windshield.

Frantic, Janae searched under the car and down the street. "Where's my daughter?"

Ethan ran up to her. "Are you all right?"

Her breathing escalated as did the pounding in her heart. "Where's Taylor?"

Lili stood behind her father and peered around his waist. "Silly Mommy, Taylor is at the party."

Falling to her knees in front of Lili, Janae gripped her shoulders and pulled her to her. "I thought he'd hit Taylor."

"Janae, are you all right?"

Her breathing slowed. That's right, Taylor wasn't even here. "Where's Ryan?"

"Right here." He stood beside the silver Corvette gaping at the injured kid.

Ethan pointed to the boy in the car. "We need to check on him. He doesn't look so good."

"He got what he deserved." She had hollered at him so many times before. "You killed my daughter. How many times have we told you to slow down, especially tonight when children are crossing back and forth?"

Ethan took her arm and pulled her back. "Sweetheart, what's going on? Both of the girls were far away from the accident."

"Well, he could have."

The kid's head bobbled, and he slumped back in his seat.

"I've got 9-1-1 on the phone," another bystander said.

Ethan held Janae's hand. "Let's take the kids home. They don't need to be here."

Janae nodded. How had she not remembered this accident? Where was her phone? The first time Grace's accident happened she'd been on the phone with Natalie's parents. She and Ethan were supposed to head to the hospital. "We need to get to the hospital."

"What?" Ethan drew his eyebrows together.

"Uh, because..." How could she explain that she'd been here before? "I had this premonition all night that something was going to happen."

Ethan shook his head. "And you think it's Taylor?"

"Well, I thought it was Taylor. I mean...you were out and then I heard the screeching." She shrugged her shoulders. "Since it wasn't her, then it has to be Grace."

"Neither of the girls were here." He took her shoulders and held her in front of him. "Are you all right?"

She nodded.

Together they walked home. When they went inside, Janae picked up her phone and saw that she'd missed several calls from Natalie's parents. Natalie's mother left a voicemail. "Grace and a couple of other kids were jumping on the trampoline and someone pushed her off. I'm taking her to Oakcrest General Hospital. It looks pretty bad."

36

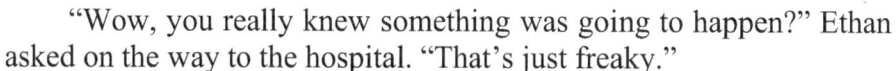

"Wow, you really knew something was going to happen?" Ethan asked on the way to the hospital. "That's just freaky."

She'd told him about her premonitions before, and he'd believed her. Shouldn't she trust him by now? "I've seen this day."

"Like in your vision or something?"

"Something." Would he believe her like he had then? "I've seen our future and our past with our children. Tonight was supposed to turn out worse."

"Our daughter is in the hospital. How is that not a horrible way to spend our evening?"

"It could have been so much worse."

As they neared the hospital, Ethan slowed the car and didn't say anything until they'd pulled into a parking space. He put his hand out to her to keep her from getting out of the car. "Is that why you were screaming for Taylor?"

Janae nodded.

"You've never had anything like this happen to you before."

Janae shook her head and chewed on the skin on the inside of her lower lip. Didn't he remember when he'd proposed to her that she'd warned him about the future? "Strange things have been happening to me. Things that if I told you, you'd want to have me committed."

He kept ahold of her hand and turned her so she was facing him. "I would never do that."

She took a deep breath. She had to tell him everything, but not now when they needed to get to Grace. "I promise I'll tell you everything when we get home."

"Promise?" The look in Ethan's eye said he wouldn't let it rest.

"Promise. Now let's go see how serious Grace's condition is."

He released her hand and Janae got out of the car.

It didn't take them long to locate Grace. By the look on her face, Janae knew her daughter was in extreme pain. Mrs. Miller was sitting in a chair beside her, while Natalie sat on the bed.

Natalie's back was to Janae. "He's such a jerk."

"Who's a jerk?" Ethan asked.

Natalie jumped as if he'd frightened her and a look of guilt crossed her face. "Oh, hey Mr. Williams."

"Mason." Grace wouldn't meet their eyes.

Mrs. Miller stood. "I'm so glad you got here so fast. We were worried when we couldn't get a hold of you."

"Thank you so much for bringing her." Ethan had turned all business.

The doctor opened the curtain and entered the small cubicle. "Are you Grace's parents?"

"Yes." Janae and Ethan answered at the same time.

"One of you will need to go to admitting so that we can get the paperwork filled out for us to treat your daughter. It looks like a Monteggia fracture, but I'll need to get an x-ray, so we can see how severe the break is."

Ethan stroked Grace's good arm. "Mom can stay with you, while I take care of all the insurance stuff."

"Come on Natalie." Mrs. Miller motioned to her daughter. "Grace's parents are here now."

Natalie leaned over the side of the bed and gave her friend a quick kiss on the forehead. "I'll see you later."

Once the others had left the room, Janae took the seat Mrs. Miller had been sitting in. "What happened?"

Grace looked down at the good hand lying in her lap.

"Was Mason there?" Of course, he had been there that night, but Grace had made up some story about how she'd accidentally fallen off the trampoline. She hoped Dylan didn't treat her daughter like this boy had.

Grace nodded.

Janae left the chair and sat on the bed. "Sweetheart, it's natural for you to like a boy. I'd be worried if you didn't. Would you believe I had a boyfriend when I was only fifteen? My parents weren't happy at all about it." She'd never shared this with her daughter for fear she'd think it was all right to have a boyfriend at her young age.

"You did? I'll bet Grandma flipped."

"She did."

"Are you going to flip if I tell you Mason is…was my boyfriend?"

"No, I'm not." Janae stroked Grace's hair being careful not to bump her injured arm. "So, tell me what happened that you ended up in the hospital emergency room on Halloween night?"

Grace looked down into her lap and then back up at Janae. "He brought another girl to the party. He said that she just needed a ride."

"So, you were a little bit jealous?"

"Not until I caught them making out on the Miller's couch in the den."

"Oh, honey, I'm sorry. Remember what we used to say about boys?"

She chuckled. "Boys are icky and yucky and not worth the testosterone they sweat in."

"Most of them." Janae tucked a lock of hair behind Grace's ear. "That doesn't explain how you broke your arm."

"I was going to call you to come and get me, but I was too embarrassed about what you would say about me meeting a boy at Natalie's house. And then Natalie convinced me to get over him. Boys aren't worth it."

Janae tried not to smile when she thought about that other boy who she would meet later and sneak off to go study with. She'd love to have another chance at handling that one better. "And then what happened?"

"We were on the trampoline, and Mason came out to apologize. He said he was just trying to get something off her mouth."

Janae raised her eyebrows. "I hope you weren't buying it."

She rolled her eyes. "I'm not stupid. I know what a make-out session looks like."

Janae just hoped Grace had never experienced one firsthand. She was much too young for that. "That's good. And then…?"

"He got up on the trampoline with us and started bouncing like nothing happened. I shoved him away from me, but he had a hold of my hand and the next thing I knew we both flew off. He landed on top of me and that's when I heard this awful sound like a branch breaking.

"Oh, baby." Janae touched her face, lifting her chin to gaze into her eyes. "I'm so sorry. Boys are such jerks."

"He didn't even check to make sure I was all right. He just ran out the side gate." A tear slid down her cheek. "I'm never liking boys again."

"Tell me that in two years when you're sixteen."

37

When they finally arrived home, Janae thanked their neighbor who'd stayed with Ryan and Lili.

"No worries." She patted Grace on the shoulder. "It's a good thing broken bones heal." Her neighbor had no clue how grateful Janae was of that fact.

After the neighbor left, Janae and Ethan helped Grace up the stairs and settled her into her bed, propping up her splinted arm. They'd have to call an orthopedic surgeon on Monday. The doctor couldn't operate anyway until the swelling went down.

Grace moaned when they adjusted her pillows. "It's hurting again."

Ethan stroked the top of her head. "I'll go get some more of the meds the doctor sent home, then I'll run to the pharmacy and fill your prescription."

"Thanks Dad, you're the best."

"I'll be back in a sec." He really was an amazing father.

Janae pulled out her phone to check the time.

"You're not going to post this on Facebook, are you?"

"Did you want me to?" Janae opened the app. Then remembering the repercussions of the last time she'd posted about Grace's arm, she closed out of her phone.

"No. I don't want Mason knowing about it."

"Then I won't." Janae slipped the phone back in her pocket.

"Really?" Grace's expression looked relieved.

"Really." That time long ago when Janae had been a lot more self-centered, she'd shared the picture of Grace in the hospital, her arm in a splint. Janae had written scathing words to the boy who'd brought on the injury. Mason had caused no end of trouble for Grace at school. Calling her names, belittling her between classes. Even his friends had joined in. Janae hadn't found out about it until Grace had come home sobbing. Until then she had borne the brunt of the harassment. Then when Janae jumped into the middle of it by going to the school and demanding that Mason be punished, did it really turn ugly. The boy's mother started attacking Janae, Grace, and anyone else who dared to think that her little boy had actually done anything wrong.

This time Grace could go back to school and face her friends. They all saw what happened. They knew. But Grace, being the girl Janae had always been proud of, would handle it with dignity.

Janae ran her hand over Grace's blond hair, loving the silky feel of it. Just like when she was little. "So, are you going to say anything to Mason?"

Grace shook her head. "No. When he sees my arm in a cast, he'll probably feel so guilty. That's the best kind of punishment."

"That's my girl. I'm so proud of you."

Ethan returned with a cup of water and an anti-inflammatory medicine and a pain killer. "Give it half an hour and you should feel better."

Grace took the pills, popped them in her mouth and washed them down. "It's a good thing it's my left arm. I can at least still do my schoolwork."

Ethan ruffled her hair. "You're amazing, did you know that?"

"Dad." She batted his hand away. "Don't mess up my hair. It's going to be hard enough to fix it with one good hand."

"All right, I'm off to the pharmacy." He straightened her locks and left the room.

"Mom..." Grace's voice trailed off.

"What can I get you?"

"I know this sounds kind of childish, but could you sleep with me tonight?"

Guilt pulled at her. The last time Grace had made this request, Janae had told her she'd be right down the hall and to call her if she needed her. Exhaustion had overcome Janae and she didn't hear Grace cry out in pain in the middle of the night. Ethan had gotten up and given her another dose of her meds.

"Anything for you." Janae turned off the light and crawled to the far side of her bed.

Grace closed her eyes. "You're the best mom."

Janae smiled and stroked her daughter's hair until she finally drifted off to sleep. "I love you, Gracie, girl," she whispered.

Ethan returned an hour later and peeked into the room, the light from the hallway cast a beam over Grace. "You sleeping here tonight?"

"I hope you don't mind."

"Of course not." He came into the room, and careful not to bump Grace, he leaned over his daughter and kissed Janae goodnight.

38

Janae stretched and then remembered not to bump Grace's arm. Odd that she hadn't awakened in the night needing more pain relief. "Grace, honey, are you alright?"

She sat up only to find herself back in her apartment in the future. She took a deep breath and pulled out her phone. Afraid to scroll through the contacts, she stared at the black screen for what felt like forever. Once she got the nerve, she unlocked her phone.

Grace.

At least she'd gotten something right and still had her daughter. Her heart beat faster and her hands grew clammy. That meant, if Grace was there, who else? She scrolled down and found Ethan, but Taylor, Ryan, and Lili were still missing.

"Wake up sunshine." Ana appeared at the foot of her bed. "Oh, you're already awake."

Janae turned her phone so that the screen faced her "I didn't lose Grace, but where are the rest of my children?"

Ana shrugged. "I'm not sure. They weren't with me in Heaven."

"Heaven?" Janae ran her hand through her tangled hair. "This is not Heaven."

"Oh, I didn't say *this* was Heaven." She turned her back on Janae and pulled the shirt and pants from the closet. "You're going to be late for work."

Janae pushed the clothes onto the floor. "I'm not going in."

"But you'll lose—"

"My job? Nope, because it will be there when I wake up here the next time."

Ana picked up the clothes and held them out to Janae. "That might be true, but then again, what happens if today is the day you wake up to tomorrow?"

Janae snatched the clothes and tossed them onto the bed. "That doesn't make sense." She went to her closet and pulled her favorite blouse and pair of jeans from their hangers. "I have more important things to take care of today. Who knows if I'll get another chance?"

Ana huffed and snapped her fingers at Janae. "Don't blame me if things go wrong. I warned you." Then she disappeared.

"Good riddance," Janae shouted, but doubted whether Ana heard her.

After a long hot shower, she dressed, blew her hair dry, and took extra time with her makeup. She retrieved her phone to call Grace and noticed she'd missed several calls. Six from her boss and one from her mother-in-law. She called Gina first.

"Where are you?" Gina's irritation came through the phone loud and clear.

"I'm not going in to work today, I'm taking Grace to lunch. I'll call Mr. Chang later and explain it."

"Janae, this is the kind of attitude that gets you fired. You're off on Sunday, take her then."

"I won't have Sunday." Janae hadn't meant to sound so angry.

Gina gasped. "You're not going to commit suicide, are you?"

"No, I'm not. It's just that, well, the most important things in life are not my job, or money or where I live. My family is the most important."

"Too bad you didn't realize that a long time ago."

"You're right. Then I'd have four children instead of just one. Gotta go." She hesitated before hanging up the phone. "Oh, and by the way, thanks for being such a good mother-in-law. I love you." She hung up before Gina could reply and then dialed Grace.

"What's wrong, Mom?" Grace's voice sounded shocked.

"Nothing. I just wanted to have lunch with my favorite

daughter. I know you're free between class and play rehearsal. Meet me at the Broken Yoke at noon."

"Okay. Who's paying? I'm a little cash short until Dad gives me my allowance."

"You're father's alive? I mean, he's okay?" Janae's heart raced. "Is he still seeing Claire?"

"Claire who?"

"Never mind. Just a funny dream I had last night. See you in a couple of hours."

"Are you all right?"

"I'm great. And don't worry about lunch. My treat."

Janae hung up before Grace could object.

Checking her banking app, Janae remembered that she didn't have enough to buy lunch. It didn't matter that she'd overdraw her bank account. It would all be right there when she woke up here again in the future, past, or wherever it was she'd end up.

Right at noon, Janae sat in the foyer of the Broken Yoke waiting for Grace. Her stomach tightened. What if she didn't show up? Maybe she should have told Grace to pick her up from work. But then that would have meant actually going into work. Wasn't her life better served by serving her daughter?

Another ten minutes passed. Grace finally came through the door. "Sorry, traffic was crazy and then there was some construction on 10th and Central."

Relieved, she stood and hugged Grace.

Her daughter stiffened. "You didn't lose another job did you?"

"No, Mr. Chang gave me the day off."

"Who?"

"Oh, that's right, you think I work for LaBaron Law Office."

"Wait, you don't?" Grace pulled her eyebrows together.

"No, I work at Charity Dollar."

"Well, at least you have a job."

The hostess came from the back of the restaurant. "I see your daughter arrived."

Janae put her arm around Grace's waist. "I'm so proud of her. She's in nursing school and in the Christmas play in a few weeks. You should come see her. She's amazing."

After the hostess seated them, Grace turned to her mother. "What was all that about?"

"Can't a mother brag?"

"It's embarrassing." Grace picked up her menu.

"Try and stay under ten dollars. I'm on a pretty tight budget." Janae perused through the selections and decided on the hamburger basket with fries. She intended to eat the entire meal. No need to box up leftovers since tomorrow would never come anyway. She'd leave the restaurant without that gnawing hunger.

"How's school going?" Janae asked, setting her menu aside.

"Most of it's not so bad. But microbiology is really hard."

"I can imagine." Janae would probably not live out the rest of the day before she got thrust back in time only to repeat the whole thing again. She didn't want to miss a moment of today without her daughter. "What are your plans for the rest of the day?"

Grace gave her an odd look. "Why?" She drew out her question.

"I'd like to hang out with you."

Grace drew her head back. "What?"

"Since I have the day off, I'd like to see what you do all day." Janae bit her tongue. What was she thinking? A young adult did not want their mother following her around. "Never mind, it was a silly idea. I think I'll go shopping."

"I have classes until three, a lab at four, after that I'm meeting someone for dinner and then I have rehearsal at six."

"You're a busy woman." Janae smiled. "I'm proud of you. Break a leg."

When they'd finished, Janae slipped her credit card in the payment folder and handed it to the waitress.

Grace stood. "I've got to get to class." She leaned over and kissed Janae on the cheek. "Thanks, Mom. This was really nice."

Janae smiled. Grace didn't hate her after all.

39

At six o'clock Janae showed up at the theater. If she wasn't going to be around for Grace's performance, then she could at least watch her rehearse. She'd sit in the very back under the cloak of darkness. Grace wouldn't even know that her mother had shown up.

When Grace, as Bess, came on stage, she took Janae by surprise. She always knew her daughter had talent, but wow, had it developed over the last five years. The poise and grace she exuded on stage was truly stunning to watch. Then her moment came, and she kissed the young Scrooge.

Dylan? That boy from high school? That couldn't be right. Hadn't she insisted they break up? She had been much too young for a boy-friend. Never mind what Grace had told her about Mason, the boy who'd knocked her off the trampoline.

Knives of irritation stabbed at her insides.

"They make a great couple, don't they?"

Janae jumped at Ana's appearance.

"I suppose, but Grace needs to finish her education before she gets involved with someone." Never mind that Dylan had become quite a handsome young man, but other character traits far outweighed good looks.

"I think they're adorable."

"Why did you decide to show up now?" Janae also didn't want Ana's opinion on her children.

"No reason. Just thought you might need a little angelic advice." Ana leaned forward and sighed. "Don't you just love young romance?"

In irritation, Janae left the auditorium and went back to her car. She stood and eyed her piece of junk. "And this is where I get in, try to start it, and end up calling my mother-in-law." She kicked the side of the car.

"Having car problems?" Dylan asked.

"I thought you were in rehearsal."

"I was, but I had to grab something from my truck real quick." He paused and eyed Janae for a moment. "Hey, you're Grace's mom."

"That would be me."

"Your daughter is amazing. I can't think of a nicer girl. It's probably because she's got such a great mother."

Suck up. "Yes, she is." Janae didn't have time for this overly handsome young man to come schmoozing up to her. Grace needed to focus on her studies.

His face turned serious. "I…well…"

"Yes." Why was he so fuddle-brained all of a sudden?

"I know that her dad is really busy and everything, and I wanted to ask him, but you're here and well…"

For someone who could memorize lines, he all of a sudden seemed at a complete loss for words. "What did you want to ask Ethan?"

"If I can marry your daughter?"

"No, you cannot!" The words flew out of her mouth before she had a chance to consider them. Did Grace love him that much? Would he take good care of her?

His face had fallen. "I know you want her to focus on her studies." Now his words practically flew out of his mouth. "I promise I won't distract her from getting her nursing degree. I'll be the best study buddy she could have. I'm working on my prerequisites for med school. We're taking a lot of the same classes. I'll be a good husband. We'll wait to have kids until after—"

Janae held up her hand stopping his monologue. "You seemed to have turned into a very nice young man. I suggest you call Mr.

Williams and speak with him directly, although, the decision rests solely with Grace."

"Then that's not a *no* from you anymore?"

"I'm reserving my judgement." Janae turned and opened her car door.

His shoulders no longer slumped when Dylan went back inside the auditorium.

What she should have done was asked him to make sure her car started. That's what a good potential son-in-law would do. She didn't want to go back inside and face a confrontation with Grace. Dylan had probably already told her she was here.

Inside the car, Janae crossed her fingers. "Please start, you bucket of bolts."

"You might ask it nicely." Ana appeared again. "Or you might even say a little prayer. You know He hasn't heard from you in a long, long, long…"

"I get it." Janae interrupted her and looked at the roof. "God, start my car."

"You might try asking nicely."

"God, please start my car?"

When nothing happened, Ana pointed to the ignition. "How about exercising a little faith and put the key back in."

Janae cast Ana a sideways glance.

"Just saying." And then she disappeared again.

After going through the same motions she'd done time after time to start the car, nothing happened. "Very funny, Ana," she muttered.

"Faith," Ana whispered back. "He can do anything."

Jane clenched her teeth. "Dear All-Powerful God who can do anything, if I'm not troubling you too much, will you please start my car?"

Before Janae could turn the key, the car started. "How did that happen?"

"Told you."

"Thank you, God?" She uttered and put the car in reverse.

Janae went back to her apartment. It was a mess. She'd left dishes in the sink, her bed was unmade, and clothes were strewn everywhere. Gathering up the clothes on the bed, Janae discovered a card. It looked familiar. Where had she seen it before? She dropped the clothes in the hamper and picked up the pink card and opened it up. Ethan's neat handwriting splayed across the entire insides.

My dearest wife,

Thank you for these wonderful years. I couldn't be a happier man than you've made me. Thanks for supporting me when my company was struggling. For helping me to hire such a wonderful staff. You deserved to be a stay at home mother. Our kids are great because of you. I can't wait to meet our son. That will even out the team.

I've made arrangements for us to get away. Be packed and ready to escape tonight.

Love forever,

Ethan

She remembered this card. It had led to that trip to San Diego—the honeymoon they never got to take. They'd spent long hours on the beach, and long nights loving each other as much as they could with her expecting a baby.

Those happy memories turned to sadness. That baby never lived. He was stillborn. The doctors had no idea what happened.

Why now? Why did this card pop up to remind her of all that she had lost? The day had been such a happy one as she packed and prepared her mother-in-law for every unforeseeable circumstance.

Gina had stood at the doorway, shooing them on their way. "I raised your husband and his brothers and sisters without killing anyone. We'll be just fine."

"You have my cell phone."

"Yes, and Ethan's."

True to her word, the children were fine when she returned home. Happier because Gina had let them get away with everything Janae scolded them about. But they were alive and that's all that mattered.

Janae held the card to her chest. She'd been in college when Ethan asked her father for her hand. Dad could have turned him down. He didn't. She guessed he could see how crazy in love she was with him... how she still was. What could she do to repair their relationship? She crawled into bed, and as she dozed off, she prayed for a brighter tomorrow.

40

Saturday, May 13, 2010

"Are you all right?" Ethan asked.

Janae rubbed her head. "What happened?"

"You bonked your head on the bottom of the desk."

She tried to sit up, but Ethan put his hand on her head to keep her from hitting the bottom side of the desk again. "What day is it?"

"Uh, Saturday."

"Saturday…Saturday?" Which Saturday? The one where they mourned the death of their son? The day after Grace's broken arm? The day they had to plan Taylor's funeral?

Ethan helped her climb out from under the desk. "You must have hit your head pretty hard."

This was the Saturday after the movers had brought all their belongings to their new home. This was the day Ryan died. Pain stabbed at her insides. "I thought I heard glass shattering." She didn't want to go downstairs and witness the blood, the sliding door in pieces. She'd imagined it well enough when Ana had told her about it.

"I didn't hear anything breaking. Are you sure?"

Janae rubbed her head where a knot was forming. "I don't know…maybe…"

"Maybe we should go down and check on the kids." Ethan held out his hand to help her up.

Janae kept a grip on his hand and followed him down the stairs.

Grace, Taylor and Ryan all sat on the couch, each with a bowl of cereal in their laps. Three pairs of eyes sat glued to the television. Janae studied her children's faces.

"Hey, you three." Janae choked, trying to keep the emotion from her voice. Ryan sat just as he had the last time.

"Hi, Mom." Ryan was the first to tear his gaze away from the screen, the look of trouble on his face. "Dad said we could eat in here cuz there's no room on the table."

"I did." Ethan looked as guilty as Ryan.

"Yeah, I know, but only for now." Janae took the bottom of his shirt and wiped the milk running down his chin.

Grace looked up for a moment. "Daddy says if it gets hot enough today, we can go swimming."

"I'll tell you what. Let's get the kitchen table cleaned off, so we can actually eat in here. Then once that's done and we've un-packed the kitchen boxes, we can all go swimming." She had their attention now.

"Yay!" All three squealed in delight.

In the process of their glee, Ryan dumped his bowl, spilling the milk. It seeped down through the crack between the cushions.

A look of dread crossed his face. "Oh, no, Mommy. I'm sorry..."

The last time they'd been in this moment, she'd scolded him for being so clumsy. This time, she took the bowl and set it on the ground, stripped off his shirt, and wiped up most of the milk. "It's okay, bud. Accidents happen, so now you understand this is why we eat at the table."

Tears welled up in his eyes. "But there's no room on the table."

Janae wiped the tears pooling on his eyelashes. "I know, and that's why you ate over here. Next time, let's eat on the floor, okay?"

Ryan wrapped his arms around Janae. "You're the best mommy ever."

"And don't you forget it." She loved the way his arms felt around her neck. If only she could capture this moment, bottle it, and bring it out to examine whenever she felt sad.

She held onto him for a few more minutes, wishing he

wouldn't pull away. "I love you," she whispered into his ear.

He didn't respond. Instead, he squirmed out of her hug, picked up his bowl, and took it to the sink. "I can clean it up all by myself."

"Yes, you can."

Grace and Taylor gaped.

Grace set her spoon in her bowl. "Wow, Mom. You must be really happy living in our new house."

Janae smiled. "Yes, I love our new house, but I love the people in it best of all."

Taylor leaned over as if to speak so that only Grace could hear. "I think Mommy is going crazy. But that's okay because crazy mommy is nicer."

A knot slugged Janae in the stomach. Had she been unkind, impatient? She shook her head. No, she was just trying to raise her children to be decent humans.

Ethan stood in the doorway, his mouth gaping.

Janae crossed over to him and closed his mouth. "I'm going to go help Daddy in his office. Can you three entertain yourselves until we're finished?"

"Okay." Ryan was searching for a rag.

"They're in the box near the sink." Janae pointed and turned to follow Ethan up the stairs.

"You really are happy about this house, aren't you?" Ethan asked.

Instead of going into the office, Janae wiggled her fingers for him to follow her into the bedroom. "I'm very happy."

A twinkle sparkled in his eye. "Are you sure you're not too sick?"

"I'm sure."

Ethan closed the bedroom door, locked it, and eyed Janae where she'd crawled onto the bed.

41

"Mom?" Pounding on the door brought Janae from her half sleep where she lay snuggled against Ethan's chest.

He leaned down and kissed her on the forehead. "Hold on. Mommy's not feeling well."

"You shouldn't lie to the kids." She brought his head down so that their lips met.

Ethan pulled away and raised his eyebrows. "You want me to tell him what we were really doing."

"Good grief, no." Janae threw on her yoga pants and pulled Ethan's t-shirt over her head.

Cracking the door a bit, Ethan asked, "What's up, bud?"

"We finished cleaning up the mess, and Grace and Taylor and me unpacked the box with the pots and pans. Can we go swimming now?"

Ethan chuckled. "I think Mommy wants all the boxes in the kitchen put away before we hit the pool."

Janae pushed Ethan into the bathroom and opened the door. "Tell everyone to go get their swimsuits on. We can unpack later."

Ryan squealed with delight. "Mom says we're going to go swimming," he hollered as he raced down the stairs.

"Who are you and what have you done with my wife?"

"She's going swimming with the kids. What are you going to do?"

He shook his head. "Not putting my computer together today?"

"That's right. Now go get your swimsuit on."

The water was a bit chillier than she normally liked it, so she didn't stay in as long as the kids. They splashed about as if they hadn't a care in the world. Ethan seemed in his domain romping with them. Once they settled in, they'd have to go to the store and buy some pool toys, especially since they were going to spend the whole summer in the backyard. Ryan turned eight in a few weeks. She knew he'd introduce himself around the neighborhood inviting everyone he met to come to his birthday party.

The baby kicked. A real one, and not just the flutters she'd been feeling for the last few weeks. She put her hand where she'd felt Liliana. How was she going to save this little one from drowning where the children would spend so many happy moments playing?

Ethan hopped out of the pool and flopped into the lounge chair beside her. "What do you think of your new house?"

"Give me a couple of weeks to move in and hang some pictures before it feels like our home." She reached over and intertwined her fingers with his. "Do you remember when we were dating, and I asked you to protect our children?"

He nodded. "I remember. I haven't forgotten."

Janae swallowed. "Our little girl, the one I'm carrying…"

"Will drown in this pool, won't she?"

She released his fingers and brought his hand to rest on her belly. "Her name is Liliana. Just before her fifth birthday…"

"I told you then that I'd do anything to protect our children."

Hot tears threatened to break free. Janae closed her eyes letting the sun sear the tears back. He'd promised twice before, and he hadn't saved them.

Ethan touched her hand. "I promise."

Janae nodded and prayed he'd save Lili. Her mind jumped forward in time—to that day. Ethan had been mowing the grass near the pool. The kids had been swimming all afternoon. Janae went in to start dinner. Lili hadn't wanted to get out.

Janae turned to latch the gate when her phone sent a notification. "Go help Daddy push the mower." She held the phone up and tried to adjust the brightness. Instagram was blowing up with all the comments and likes on her post about her latest decorating project.

Before scrolling through the comments, she hollered at Ethan,

"Watch Lili!"

His head bobbed once.

Lili tugged on his pant leg.

Janae had watched them for a moment before going into the house.

Her other three children had scattered to their rooms.

Janae had pulled the Insta-Pot from the cupboard, the chicken from the fridge and began the meal prep.

Not long after, the lawnmower quit, and Ethan came in the back door. "That smells delicious."

"Where's Lili?" Janae asked, stirring the green beans where she was sautéing them.

Ethan glanced around the room. "I thought she came inside."

"No, she was mowing the lawn with you." Janae scrunched her forehead.

"That lasted two minutes."

Janae's stomach twisted.

Everything had moved in slow motion.

Finding Lili at the bottom of the pool.

Ethan jumping in.

Janae calling 911.

The paramedics arriving.

The ride in the ambulance.

The pronouncement of her death at the hospital.

Janae screaming.

At Ethan.

The funeral.

Finally, her marriage slowly dissolving over the next three months.

42

Friday, Dec 13, 2019

Janae must have dozed where she'd been sitting beside the pool. She jerked awake and brought her hand over her eyes to block out the sun. Why hadn't she been watching the children? Where was Ethan?

No, she couldn't be...

She took her arm away from her eyes.

Her apartment.

With a feverish pitch, she searched her contacts. There was Ethan, Grace, Ryan, Taylor, her work. No Liliana. But then, did a nine-year-old need a phone?

She dialed Ethan's phone.

"We're sorry, the number you have dialed is no longer in service."

Ugh! She'd forgotten.

She dialed her oldest daughter. "Grace?"

"Hi, Mom."

"Did Lili die?"

The silence on the other end confirmed her fear. Ethan hadn't saved Lili after all.

"I'm sorry, honey. I'm not feeling well."

"Did you take your meds?" Grace asked.

Janae shook her head. "Yes. I'm sorry I bothered you. I need to get ready for work."

"Can I meet you for lunch? Will Mr. LaBaron let you have an extra hour?"

"Sure that would be great. The little Italian restaurant around the corner from Charity Dollar?"

"Okay, see you then…"

Janae pulled the phone from her ear to end the call.

"Mom?"

She brought the phone back. "Yeah?"

"I love you." Grace hung up.

"I love you, too," Janae said to the dead air. That was odd. Grace had never said that before. What had changed since Lili's death and her life now? Maybe she could ask her later.

Ana appeared at the closet and pulled out the blue shirt and black pants. "Oh! I see you're already awake. You've been doing that a lot lately."

Janae took the clothes from her. "Ana, if Ethan didn't save Lili, then why am I still here?"

"Because it's not Ethan who needs to save Lili."

Janae stepped into the bathroom, peeled off her pajamas and slipped her work clothes on. "I don't understand," she said through the open door.

"It's not Ethan who needs to save Lili," Ana repeated.

Flipping her hair into a ponytail she looked into the mirror. "I don't know CPR, and the paramedics arrived too late."

"That's not what I meant." Ana held out Janae's phone.

Janae took the phone and stared at it for a moment. "What has this got to do with anything?"

"It will come to you." Ana disappeared.

"What? No toast? No juice?"

Janae finished getting ready for work and hurried out the door. Starting the car was easy this morning. She uttered a quick prayer. "Thank you, Dear Father in Heaven. Do you think you could start it again tonight?"

The icy patch was still in the parking lot. Janae went around it. "I'm here," she said as she entered the store.

Mr. Chang looked up from the boxes he was shelving. "You early today."

"I wanted to put in an extra hour if I can take a little longer during my lunch break." She walked to the back office not waiting for Mr. Chang to reply. After putting on her apron, she went to the front of the store.

The door chimed and Mr. Chang nodded to the customers. "You help them. I do this."

Janae went to the young mother with a child on one hip and the other with her hand clutched firmly in hers. "Can I help you find something?" She knew exactly what the woman wanted.

"I'd like to find something the kids can take to their father." She shifted the child on her hip.

"My daddy's in jail," the older one piped up.

"He's not in jail now. He was released last week and is in a halfway house until he's cleared by his probation officer to come home."

Janae led her to the aisle where the survival kit was. "Let's see what we can find." She held out the item, and the woman's face lit up.

"It's just like the one I saw on Amazon." She took the package from Janae and turned it over, looking for the price tag. Her face fell when she saw it. "Maybe we'll just get him a package of Tootsie Rolls. They're his favorite."

Janae took the kit from her, walked to the cash register, grabbing a large bag of the candy on the way.

The woman hurried to catch up to Janae. "But I can't afford that."

"I know." If this was her life now, she planned on making it count. She bent down to the little boy. "What do you want for Christmas?"

"A stomp rocket," he said without hesitation.

"Did you ask Santa Claus for one?" Janae asked.

He nodded.

"Then I'm sure that's exactly what you'll find under your tree." She grabbed a large brown bag. "I'll be right back." Janae walked down the toy aisle. After locating the item, she stuffed it in the bag, then picked out a toy appropriate for a baby and set it next to the stomp rocket."

She didn't return to the front counter right away but went to the back office where Mr. Chang sat at his desk. "I'm going to purchase a few things for a nice lady. I know there's not enough in my bank account to cover it. Would it be possible to take it out of next week's paycheck?"

Mr. Chang examined her for a moment. "What is total?"

"Just a little over forty."

He nodded. "Out of your pay."

"Thank you." As a second thought, Janae grabbed her thick coat and hurried back to the front of the store, hoping the lady hadn't left yet.

The woman still stood at the counter, her wallet open, she shuffled through a few bills in one of the pockets. "I only have eight dollars." She held out a five, two ones and a handful of change.

"Perfect, that's exactly how much everything costs." Janae put in the zero dollars and zero cents into the register. "Oh, and here's your change." She slipped the money the woman had given her back into her hand. Then quietly so the little boy couldn't hear, she said, "I hope he's worth it and is willing to make significant changes." She then handed her coat to the woman. "It's too cold outside for this thin jacket you're wearing."

The woman's eyes filled with tears as she slipped on the coat and took the bags. "Thank you so much."

When the door chimed signaling the woman's departure, Janae looked up at the ceiling. "My good deed."

Mr. Chang stood at the end of the aisle. "You can't help everybody who needs help."

"I know." Janae's bank account wouldn't allow it. But for today, one woman's Christmas just got a little brighter.

43

When Janae walked into the restaurant, Grace had already been seated.

"Where's your coat?" she asked.

"I forgot it at home." Janae didn't want to go about tooting her own horn. Hadn't she heard once that in proclaiming one's good deed, the reward was already allocated in the praise of the world?

"Well, that was kind of dumb."

Janae shrugged. "Yeah, it was."

Lunch with Grace went much better than Janae had hoped for. This was the daughter she remembered—animated, enthusiastic, and happy. In spite of losing her sister, Grace seemed to have moved on. Now that she examined her daughter, hers was the face of a girl in love. That boy…Dylan, the one who'd approached her in the parking lot. He was handsome, for sure, but there had to be more to a man than his good looks. He had to be smart if he was a premed student.

Maybe the reason Janae had resented Dylan so much was because of Grace's age. Sixteen was too young to get wrapped up in a boy. But Grace was almost twenty-one. Janae had been about that age when Ethan proposed to her. Maybe it wouldn't be such a bad thing.

"So, Dylan, huh?" Janae asked between bites.

Color erupted on Grace's face. "He's super nice and smart and funny and…"

"I know," Janae interrupted her. "You're in love with that boy, aren't you?"

"More than ever."

"I'm sorry I underestimated him." Janae reached across the table and put her hand on Grace's. "You'd be stupid not to snatch him up."

Grace wrapped her fingers around her mother's hand. "Then you don't mind so much that I want to marry him."

"Maybe a little. I am losing my oldest daughter."

"Mom, you've heard the saying, 'A son is yours until he takes a wife, but a daughter is yours all of her life.'"

Janae had no idea what had happened since the last time she'd met Grace for lunch. Maybe things weren't as bad even though they'd still lost Lili. What if she wasn't supposed to save Lili after all…

Grace pulled her hands back and took another bite of her pasta. "Dylan and I are in the show together. You should come and say hello."

"Tonight?"

"I was thinking after the show. I can get you a ticket if you'd like. Probably not on the same night that Dad is coming."

"Is he bringing Claire?"

Grace took a sip of her water. "I have no idea."

"So, are they having an office fling?" Janae paused. That wasn't right. She'd decided not to hire Claire for this very reason.

"What are you talking about?" Grace asked.

"Didn't I hire Claire to work for your dad?"

"No, they met at church."

"Church?" Since when had Ethan gotten religious?

"Yeah, he started going after you guys divorced. That's where he met Claire."

"Huh." Pangs of jealousy shot through Janae. Was there a way to get her husband back? "Are they dating?"

Grace shrugged. "I don't know. I've been too busy to keep up with his..." she paused.

Janae could tell her daughter was struggling with how to explain Claire. "Love life," Janae finished.

Grace looked down at her hands. "Dad never stopped loving you."

"Then why is he dating Claire?"

"He's lonely, Mom. You don't expect him to just sit around, do you?"

"But he doesn't love her. He loves me."

Sadness took over her face. "You told him you never wanted to see him or hear from him again."

That's why he changed his phone number. "Do you think he'd talk to me?"

"You can try."

44

It hadn't been easy to convince Mr. Chang to extend Janae's lunch. She would have even risked getting fired if he hadn't agreed. Thirty minutes was all Janae needed.

Janae paced the sidewalk in front of the home he was building. The two-story structure sprawled with its craftsman columns.

He finally came out the front door. His hair had touches of gray, but his blue eyes nearly pierced her when he stopped, a scowl spreading across his face. "You're not Grace."

"I'm sorry I had her deceive you like that." She tucked a lock of hair behind her ear.

"I thought you never wanted to cross paths again."

Janae knew him better than anyone else. His words were his defense mechanism that kept him from showing his true feelings. She'd hurt him so deeply that there would be no repairing the breech.

"Why are you here?" He folded his arms.

"I... well..." She could feel her resolve fading faster than marshmallows in raspberry hot chocolate.

"Grace always hoped that we'd get back together again. Is that why she put you up to this?"

"No...Ethan. I asked her to call you and pretend she was going to meet you because..."

He ran his hand through his hair and turned to go back into the house.

"Wait." Janae ran after him.

When he turned back to face her, the pain on his face was fleeting, until he'd steeled it without emotion. "We had our chance."

"I know." She touched his arm, and he flinched. That single gesture shot daggers into Janae's heart. "I just wanted you to know I'm sorry."

"Sorry for what?" Hurt hung thick in his voice.

"I'm sorry for blaming you for Lili's death, for all the anger and animosity I had for you."

Ethan stared at her like she was some kind of alien who come to perform experiments on him.

When he didn't say anything, Janae continued, "I hope you'll have a happy marriage and that she'll be a better wife than I ever was." She turned to go back to her car.

"Janae…" he called after her.

She fought the tears for control and lost miserably. How could she embarrass herself by turning around to face him?

He caught up to her and pulled her arm around to stop her. "I…" He reached out and wrapped his arms around her. "I…I'm sorry, too."

"Ethan?" Claire came down the front steps.

Ethan released Janae and turned back to his fiancée. "Sorry, I was just…"

Claire glared at Janae. "Who's this?"

"This is…Janae." He said it as if he was embarrassed to get caught with his ex.

"Oh." Claire held out her hand. "Nice to meet you." She said the words with all the formality expected in an awkward situation. Then she turned back to Ethan. "The painters want to know if this is the right shade."

"You decide. You're the one who has to live with it."

Janae tried to keep her eyes on Claire's face, but she couldn't help the quick glance down at her protruding belly.

Claire huffed. "I want everything perfect for when we get back from our honeymoon."

"I'll be in in a second."

Claire turned, jogged up the steps and went back in the house. A money digger. Janae understood. No wonder he didn't help much with Janae's finances. Probably at her insistence.

"Janae…it's not…" Ethan's face grew warm.

"I wish you the best." Janae couldn't stand to hear about his up-coming marriage. She turned and raced to her car and watched Ethan disappear behind the double doors.

"I love you, Ethan…" The searing tears slipped down her cheeks.

45

Janae tried starting the car with the same results as always. She hated to go back up to the house and ask for Ethan's help.

"God?" Hey, it had worked before.

"I'm kind of stuck again… and…"

Ana tapped on the window. "Having trouble?"

Janae rolled it down. "Yes, just like always."

"You should go ask Ethan to help."

Janae's eyebrows shot up. "Right. With Claire breathing down his neck? I don't think so."

"You've discovered a few things about him, haven't you?"

"That I'm still madly, crazy, insanely in love with him, yes." Janae realized she never wanted the divorce. Why had she even uttered those horrible words?

"Then go ask for his help." Ana opened the door and motioned for Janae to get out.

"I don't think…"

"Just go." Ana pointed up the walkway.

Taking a deep breath, Janae turned and went to the front door again, then rang the bell.

Ethan answered the door. Surprise mingled with confusion crossed his face.

"I can't get my car started, and I have to be back to work in fifteen minutes." Janae had no idea how this was going to help. If anything, it would just make Claire more upset. Except, why should Janae worry about Claire's feelings? Janae had been married to him first.

"Did you try pumping the gas?" he asked.

"If you knew how many times, you'd think I'd flooded the…"

"Your car doesn't have a carburetor."

"Oh, then why does it work to pump the gas pedal?"

Ethan shrugged. "Let me check something." He didn't wait for her to follow him back to her car. He moved the seat back to accommodate his long legs. "First of all, make sure your headlights and your heater are off."

"I always turn the lights off." Janae was smart enough to know that interior lights left on would drain the battery. The heater she'd left on.

He shut the blower motor off. "Next you have to turn the key to the on position and wait until all the dash lights quit flashing. See?" He pointed to the dashboard. Once the lights had all gone off, Ethan turned the ignition. It sounded like it wanted to start with the noise it was making.

"That's what it was doing this morning." And every other morning she'd awakened in this time-period.

He got out of the car and opened the hood. "Let me check something." He wiggled a few cables and wires. Finally, he pulled a loose thingy and held it up. "This is your problem."

"Okay. What is it?"

"You have a couple of spark plugs that need to be replaced. It wouldn't hurt to replace them all."

Her heart sunk. She couldn't afford that. "Thanks."

Even under his heavy jacket, Ethan still had his broad shoulders. "Meet me tomorrow at Auto Palace, and I'll take care of it."

She'd just made crazy, passionate love to him yesterday…well, what felt like yesterday. Desperately, she wanted to press her body against his, feel the warmth of his skin, the caress of his kisses, the connection they'd once had. She cleared her throat. "I can take care of it with my next paycheck."

Janae got into her car and tried starting it the way Ethan had showed her. It sputtered a couple of times before turning over. "Thank you," she said through the open window.

He leaned his arms on the windowsill, his breath warm on her cheek. She turned her head, their lips precariously close. All she had to do was lean toward him a few inches. Did she dare?

As if someone pushed her from behind, her mouth connected with his. He reached his hand behind her neck and pulled her closer, deepening the kiss. She responded to him as she always had, wanting more.

Slowly he drew away from her, leaving her breathless. He cleared his throat. "I'll see you tomorrow."

He turned and went up the sidewalk.

Janae didn't think she'd need to turn on the heater as she drove back to Charity Dollar. His kiss would leave her warm all day. If only tomorrow would come and she could win Ethan away from Claire.

"Told you." Ana said. "He's still in love with you."

"How do I fix this?"

Ana was gone again. Why couldn't she stay around long enough to answer simple questions?

46

Janae spent the rest of her shift helping customers and ringing up their purchases.

Mr. Chang came from the back of the store where he was helping one last customer. Janae remembered her from the last time she'd come in. Her hollow cheeks, her vacant eyes. This was a horrible time to be homeless.

Her boss set the packages of gravy mix, instant potatoes, and a can of beef chunks on the counter. "You ring up zero dollars."

Tears filled the woman's eyes. "Please, no. I can pay for the ramen." She pulled out two quarters and laid them on the counter.

Her boss pushed the quarters back to the woman. "And she take the noodles with her, too."

Janae put the items in a bag and added a couple napkins, a fork, and spoon. "Wait here." She raced to the back room and returned with several pieces of tin foil.

"Thank you." The woman stuffed the foil in the bag along with the other items.

"Where's your shelter?" Janae asked.

She nodded. "It's not far."

"Do you have bus fare?" Janae had no cash on her and hoped the woman said yes.

"I can walk. It's not far."

Determined not to let the woman go out into the freezing cold, Janae said, "I'm almost done, I can drive you."

The woman tucked the bag under her arm. "I'm fine." Then before Janae could argue, the woman headed toward the door. Janae had to catch her before she left the store.

When she reached the woman, Janae touched the woman's shoulder. "You sit right here, and I'll be with you in just a few minutes."

She started to object, but Janae put up her hand. "I won't take no for an answer."

Mrs. Chang came from the back room and carried the cash drawer to the office to count the night's take.

Janae wrapped the scarf around her neck and shivered when she opened the door. "Good night, Mr. Chang."

"You be early tomorrow. It's a bigger day."

Two Saturdays before Christmas. Janae nodded. "I'll be here, unless I get sent back in time—again."

"You be on time."

"Of course." Janae held the door open for the woman and they stepped into the cold.

"Where's your coat?" The woman asked.

"I was late for work, and I left it at home. Once we get the heater cranked up, I'll be fine." She hoped her car would start. Janae pointed across the parking lot. "I'm that Honda over there."

Once she'd unlocked the car, the woman hesitated before getting in. "You're sure this is no trouble."

"Not at all." Janae held out her hand. "I'm Janae."

"Christine." She shook Janae's hand.

"It's nice to meet you."

The car roared to life on the first try. "I've been having trouble getting it started." She took a deep breath. "Thank you, Ethan."

"Usually, I thank God for little miracles like that."

Janae smiled. "I already thanked Him this morning. My ex gave it a temporary fix-it this afternoon."

Christine pulled her scarf higher around her neck. "Still, God sends people in our path who help us to see important things."

If Janae didn't know better, Christine could have been referring to Ana.

"Let's get the engine warmed up so we don't have to sit here in the cold." Janae revved the gas, before putting it into reverse.

"I really appreciate this." The sack in her lap crunched. "I probably missed dinner, so this food will come in handy."

The drive to the shelter took longer than Janae had imagined. Now she was glad she'd given the woman a ride. How could Christine have made it without freezing to death?

Janae pulled into a parking spot outside the women's shelter. "Good luck with everything."

Christine got out of the car and headed up the walkway to the front door. Again, Janae put the car in reverse. With the long day Janae had had, she just wanted to fall into bed and sleep.

Ana spoke from the back seat. "Wait to make sure she gets inside all right."

Janae startled. "You've got to stop jumping in like that."

"Sorry."

Christine opened the door and went in.

"Oh, good." Janae took her foot off the brake and backed out.

"Wait. It looks like she's coming back out."

Christine watched the door close, put her arm on the glass and her head on her arm. The slump of her shoulders said that there were no beds available.

"What should I do?" Janae asked.

Ana was gone.

Typical.

Janae couldn't let the woman stay out in the cold or walk to another shelter. How many were there in the vicinity?

She rolled down the window. "Christine?"

Startled, the woman turned.

"Come on, get in."

With hesitation, she came down the walkway and got back in the car. "There's a shelter on 7th Street."

Janae took her to three more shelters, and in each one the beds were also gone. She couldn't just turn the woman out into the cold, and yet her apartment was never meant for more than one person. She chewed her lip for a moment. "Do you have any family?"

Christine barely nodded.

"Can I take you there?" Janae asked.

"I don't know if they'll want to see me." Christine's head hung as if ashamed.

"You might be surprised." Janae hadn't thought Ethan would ever want to see her again, but that kiss this afternoon said otherwise. "Would you like to try?"

She nodded and chewed on her thumb nail.

When they arrived at the neighborhood where Janae used to live, she took a deep breath. It was like coming home, but not being welcomed. Is this how Christine felt?

They stopped at her son's house. The same car that had hit and killed Taylor was parked outside. Her heart dropped to her shoes, and she didn't know if she could get out of the car. "That car…" Janae pointed to the Chevy Corvette. "Is that your son's?"

"My grandson." Christine kept her hand on the handle as if she, too, was afraid to leave the warmth of the car.

Janae searched Christine's face. "He drives too fast."

"Yes, he does. I've talked to my grandson about it several times, but he won't listen." Her eyes never left the front door where an ornate pine wreath hung. The white lights trimming the eaves were warm and inviting.

"Do you want me to go to the door with you?"

She turned her gaze away from the house and took ahold of Janae's hand. "Would you, please? I don't think I can face him alone."

Janae squeezed her hand in return. "Well, let's go." She understood the fear of seeing her family again after so much had passed.

Wrapping the scarf tighter around her shoulders, Janae exited the car. The cold air sent shivers of icy fingers through her sweater, a reminder of her good deed earlier in the day.

When Christine didn't ring the bell, Janae did.

A young child hollered, "I'll get it."

The door flew open. The little boy, maybe ten or eleven stood staring for a few minutes before flinging himself into Christine's arms. "Grandma! It's Grandma. She's here."

"Mom?" A man about the same age as Janae stopped on the landing, then raced down the rest of the stairs and scooped up Christine. "We've been so worried about you."

"Oh, Michael, I'm so sorry." Her muffled voice barely carried where he held her against his chest. "I shouldn't have interfered."

"No, I should have listened." Michael set her down and held her at arm's length. "Benji…" his voice choked up. "It's bad, Mom."

"Where is he?"

"He's in jail. He was involved in an accident, and he tried to run from the police."

As if just now noticing Janae, Michael looked at her. When he didn't say anything, Christine gestured to her. "This is Janae. She encouraged me to come home."

Michael held out his hand. "Thank you for finding my mother."

47

Janae crawled into bed. Her car brought her safely home. The card she'd found the other night lay on her nightstand.

No Ana.

If she stayed awake all night, would she get to see Ethan the next day at the auto parts store? Even though she desperately wanted to see her husband again, exhaustion was claiming its toll on her body.

She did a few jumping jacks, took a shower, stretched, and played a mindless game on her phone, anything to keep from falling asleep.

Bored, she set her phone on top of the card. Her mind wandered to all the places they'd been together—the short trip to Cancun, the vacation with the kids to Disneyland, the hike down to the bottom of the Grand Canyon.

She picked up her phone and thumbed through the photos, glad she'd saved them years ago on the cloud. Most of the pictures were selfies of her and the children, her and Ethan, her and… Why had she taken so many of herself? Had she really been so self-centered?

Going through each of her social media accounts made her stomach tighten with self-loathing. A plethora of adjectives to describe her ran through her head: conceited, stuck up, cocky, big headed, phony, arrogant, narcissistic. Each post had been about Janae, not her family, not her life, just her and her accomplishments.

She swallowed.

She shut off her phone and laid it face down on the nightstand.

Visions of the day Lili died echoed around her like a haunting ghost.

"Go help Daddy push the mower." Janae turned to latch the gate when her phone sent a notification. She held it up and tried to adjust the brightness. Instagram was blowing up with all the comments and likes on her earlier post.

Before scrolling through them, she had hollered at Ethan, "Watch Lili!"

His head bobbed once.

Lili tugged on his pant leg.

Janae had checked her phone again.

I love your new entry table

Super cute organization

Can you come help me with mine?

How fun to be able to redo. I need more $$$

Janae looked up when Ethan came through the sliding glass door. "I thought Lili was helping you mow the lawn."

"That lasted two minutes."

Janae's stomach had twisted as everything moved in slow motion until...*finding Lili at the bottom of the pool.*

Ethan jumping in.

Janae calling 911.

The paramedics arriving.

The ride in the ambulance.

The pronouncement of her death at the hospital.

Janae screaming.

At Ethan.

The funeral.

Her mind went back to that moment at the gate. How could she have stopped it from happening? Janae had turned to latch the gate... turned to latch the gate...turned to...adjust the brightness on the phone... then checking the notifications on Instagram.

Latch the gate.

Didn't she?

Oh, no...it couldn't be her fault. She'd latched the gate... hadn't she?

She watched her hands checking Instagram. They had never touched the latch.

No.

Lili had gotten bored with helping Ethan. She never wanted to get out of the pool, so she went through the unlatched gate. Slipped into the pool…

Hot tears ran down Janae's cheeks. "I killed Lili…" she said through her sobs. "It wasn't Ethan's fault. Why had I blamed him?"

Janae would have cried herself to sleep if a sharp knock on the door hadn't brought her fully awake.

Through the peephole, she saw Ethan standing on the other side.

"Just a minute." Janae blew her nose and tried to wipe the residue of grief from her eyes before she opened the door.

Ethan stood there for a moment. "May I come in?"

She nodded and stepped out of the way, then closed the door.

"About this afternoon…"

Janae put her hand over his mouth. "It was my fault."

"The car? Probably. You should have taken it in when you first had trouble with it starting…"

"No. Lili's death."

Ethan didn't say anything.

"You knew I didn't latch the gate, didn't you?"

He still didn't say a word.

"Why? Why didn't you tell me?"

His hands on her shoulders surprised her. "What good would it have done to place blame? You were already hurting because our daughter was gone."

Her heart seized. He'd let her put the accusation on him. "It was my fault, and you didn't say a word."

"It was an accident."

The moan welling up inside her broke free and she slumped. Ethan lifted her in his arms and set her on the bed and sat beside her. His gentle rocking didn't soothe her, but only drove the guilt and anguish deeper. No wonder he'd let her go. She'd been so shameless and cruel with her accusations. She shouldn't have been worth the fight. Janae didn't blame him for divorcing her.

Yet, here he was, holding her like he always had when she needed him, even right after Lili's death.

Ana appeared beside Ethan. "Silly Janae, you see, he still loves you.

He'd take you back in a heartbeat… if you'll let him."

"But how can he ever forgive me."

"He already has. You need to forgive yourself."

Ethan stroked her cheek, his fingers lingering on her jaw. "Who are you talking to?"

"Ana…" she gestured to where her guardian angel stood.

Ethan turned. "I don't see anyone."

Maybe only Janae could see her. "It doesn't matter."

"Did you mean Liliana?"

Janae's head snapped up.

Ana smiled, the dimple prominent on her cheek. Why hadn't Janae noticed it before?

"Liliana?"

Ana nodded and then disappeared.

"I wish I'd never divorced you," she whispered. "And now you're getting married." The tears gathered and flowed down her face.

"Where did you get that idea?" Ethan touched her chin with his thumb before brushing at her tears.

"Grace said you were marrying Claire. You built a new house for her."

"I'm not marrying her. She and her fiancé are building that house."

"But I thought…"

"I never wanted anyone but you." Ethan kissed her until her toes curled and her stomach tingled. The last residue of grief disappeared like whipped cream in raspberry hot chocolate before she drifted off to sleep, safe in his arms.

48

In an instant, like someone had taken a picture with a bright flash, Janae stood at the gate to the swimming pool.

"But I don't want to get out," Lili whined.

"There's nobody to watch you." Janae bent down to eye-level with her daughter.

Lili stomped her foot. "I can watch myself." When had she started that trait?

Janae wrapped the towel around Lili's shoulders. "The rule is, 'nobody swims alone." She pointed to Ethan. "Go help Daddy push the mower." Janae turned to latch the gate when her phone sent a notification. She held it up and tried to adjust the brightness. Instagram was blowing up with all the comments and likes on her earlier post.

Before scrolling through them, she hollered at Ethan, "Watch Lili!"

His head bobbed once.

Lili raced across the lawn and tugged on his pant leg.

He put her on his feet while she gripped the handle.

Janae turned back to her phone, looked at it for less than a moment without opening the notification tab. She looked back at Lili, back at her phone.

She latched the gate, making sure the lock was in place.

Once more she looked down at her phone.

Then she
    pitched it
    into
    the pool.

Epilogue

Summer passed too fast as did autumn before winter blew in cold and biting. With Christmas a few days away, Janae breathed in the smell of the pine tree wafting through the house. She fluffed the pillows and glanced at her pristine nightstand and then over at Ethan's messy dresser top.

Thankful he provided this beautiful home for her, she gathered up the receipts and took them into the den. She'd get them scanned tomorrow.

Grace tapped on the door jam. "Hey, Mom, I was wondering..." Her blouse was still a lot lower than Janae was comfortable with.

Janae set the bin next to the document reader.

Grace slid the notebook higher up her chest until it reached her chin. "I just felt kind of ugly when I got home."

"Uh-huh. When do you worry about your looks around Natalie?" Even if everything turned out all right in the future, Janae still had to set standards. "Will Dylan be there?"

A soft huff escape Grace. "That's what I came to talk to you about."

"Dylan?"

"Yeah. His parents are going to help serve dinner at a homeless shelter on Christmas day, and he invited me to come."

"On one condition."

Shock registered across Grace's face. "What...?"

Janae crossed to where Grace stood. "He has to come have Christmas Eve dinner with us."

"That's it?"

Janae smiled. "I have a feeling we'll be seeing a lot more of him in the future."

Grace wrapped her arms around Janae. "Thanks, Mom. You're the best."

"And don't you forget it."

The front door closed. "Janae?"

"In your office," she called down to Ethan.

He took the stairs two at a time holding a small package. "Guess what came at the office today?" He held the box out to her.

"Why didn't you just put it under the tree?"

"Claire says I should give it to you now." He held it out to her.

Grace nudged Janae's arm. "Go ahead, Mom…can't you see how excited he is to give it to you."

Janae's eyes went from Ethan to her daughter and then to the box. She pulled at the ribbon. "Did Claire wrap it?"

"She took extra care to make sure it was perfect."

The wrapping fell away, and an iPhone box sat in the palm of Janae's hand. "Ah Ethan, you didn't need to do this. I'm quite content with my cheap phone."

"Since you dropped your phone in the pool…I didn't want you to go without."

"Oh, cool." Grace held out her hand. "You want me to set it up for you?"

Janae handed the phone over to Grace. How did she explain to Ethan that she hadn't dropped it, but tossed it, and her life had been better without it? Instead, she wrapped her arms around his neck. "All I want this year is my family."

Lili raced up the stairs and threw her arms around her parents. "Silly Mommy, we're right here."

About the Author

Betsy Love grew up in Tucson, Arizona where she met DeWalt, the love of her life, at church when she was 7 years old. By the age of 13, she told all her friends that she would one day marry him. Oh, such doubters. By the time she reached 18, her dreams came true when he asked her for a date. One year later, Betsy proved all the naysayers wrong and married him!

They have 20 grandchildren, who are the joy of her life, although, you should see their faces really light up when they see their grandpa.

Now residing in Linden, Arizona, she enjoys much cooler days than her thirty plus years in the Mesa/Gilbert area.

When not writing you can find her binge-watching Korean romance/drama shows and playing World of Warcraft with her husband.

She vows to try gardening one more time, next spring, after the last frost in her new mountain home.

You can connect with her at:

Website: www.betsylove.com

Facebook:https://www.facebook.com/Betsy-Love-Author-209463519104404

Twitter: @betsyloveauthor

Email: authorbetsylove@gmail.com

Parler: @betsylove

www.ingramcontent.com/pod-product-compliance
Lightning Source LLC
Chambersburg PA
CBHW060916180626
46817CB00004B/1282

* 9 7 8 1 7 3 5 7 0 4 9 1 3 *